SING TO ME

ALSO BY JESSE BROWNER

SING

TO

ME

JESSE BROWNER

LITTLE, BROWN AND COMPANY

New York Boston London

Little, Brown and Company
Hachette Book Group
1290 Avenue of the Americas, New York, NY 10104
littlebrown.com

First Edition: May 2025

Little, Brown and Company is a division of Hachette Book Group, Inc. The Little, Brown name and logo are trademarks of Hachette Book Group, Inc.

The publisher is not responsible for websites (or their content) that are not owned by the publisher.

The Hachette Speakers Bureau provides a wide range of authors for speaking events. To find out more, go to hachettespeakersbureau.com or email hachettespeakers@hbgusa.com.

Little, Brown and Company books may be purchased in bulk for business, educational, or promotional use. For information, please contact your local bookseller or the Hachette Book Group Special Markets Department at special.markets@hbgusa.com.

Book interior design by Marie Mundaca

ISBN 978-0-316-58123-3
Library of Congress Control Number: 2024946406

Printing 1, 2025

LSC-C

Printed in the United States of America

To JC

And something miraculous brushes up
Against the filth and the ruin,
something no one, no one, has known,
though we have sought it so long.

Anna Akhmatova

SING TO ME

"SING, FROGS!"

Hani scans the horizon of the pond through the bulrushes. It's been a long while since he's had time to hunt frogs, but it's not a skill you forget, especially when you've been doing it ever since you can remember. He was always good at it—good at keeping still and good at creeping up barefoot behind them—even when he was barely more than a toddler and had to compete with the older boys, who never let him win at anything and never wasted a chance to remind him of how small and pathetic he was. All those boys are gone now, his brothers and their friends, and most of them will probably never come back, but the frogs have been plentiful ever since the last of the wading birds were eaten or scared away. It feels like years since Hani last saw an egret, a stork, or a heron. Now he has the frogs all to himself, just as the spring floods are cresting and mating season is in full

3

voice. A boy frog singing his heart out, or a girl frog in love with the beauty of his song, will barely notice the approach of a cunning hunter, even one as large as an eleven-year-old boy.

"Sing to me now, you frogs who hold the shores of the pond!"

Hani crouches behind one now and scoops it up in both hands. Resigned to its fate, it does not struggle as he grasps both hind legs in his fist and swings it in a looping, overhead arc against the flat stone that he has brought with him for that purpose. The frog's skull cracks against the stone and Hani slips the limp corpse into the hemp sack slung across his shoulder, heavy with prey. Even as a little boy, Hani took no pleasure in killing harmless creatures or showing off his hunting skills the way the other boys did, but this is no child's game he's about to embark on. This is serious business, a man's business, as Father might call it. He squints up at the cloud-veiled sky and decides that the afternoon is far enough along to call it quits for the day. He rises from his squat, grabs the stone, and heads for higher ground, free of reeds, where he drops the stone and empties the bag beside it. He counts twenty-three frogs in total. He hopes they'll see him through the first leg of his journey, but the truth is he has absolutely no idea what lies ahead. Seeing as how he barely even knows where he's going or what hidden dangers lie in the way, the question of whether he has enough smoked frog legs to get him there is likely to be the least of his worries.

The family's only bronze dagger is too precious to use for anything but slaughtering livestock and sacrificing sheep, and in any case Father took it with him when he went away, but Hani's flint blade with the bone handle is more than sharp enough for the job. He plops a frog on the stone, belly down, and saws off its feet. He makes a shallow gash across its back from shoulder to shoulder, holds the frog's head against the stone with his left hand, and peels the skin away from the flesh with his right, rolling it down the length of the torso in one smooth movement until it pops off the legs, inside out. He cuts through the two bones of the lower back, splits the carcass in half at the hips, and flings the inedible portion over his shoulder into the water. Using a sturdy cattail sharpened to a point at one end, he skewers the thighs at the top, where they meet at the crotch. Once he has repeated this task twenty-three times, Hani has a string of frog thighs hanging from the bowed reed like a necklace of glistening ruby pendants, and the earth beneath his feet is spongy with blood. He washes his hands, the knife, and the stone in the pond, then proceeds uphill and along a winding path to the farmhouse. He suspends the cattail over the hearth fire in two notches cut into the chimney stone, where the kettle used to hang. Father took that with him, too. Hani flops down onto the three-legged stool by the hearth, tipping it to rest his back against the warm stone.

The room is not big, but on cloudy days like this it can be so murky that the far corners are lost in shadow. There's only the one doorway to the outside and a narrow slit for a window. There's an opening in the roof above the hearth to allow the smoke to escape, and another doorway to the room where the family used to sleep, all six of them and the dogs in the winter. It's hard to believe that they somehow all managed to cram themselves in here not so long ago, together with the long table and benches that were chopped up for firewood several years back. Now there's nothing left but this stool, the frog legs roasting over the fire, and the rucksack that Hani has prepared for his journey. And Hani himself, of course. When he's gone, and the sheep have been let loose to roam and fend for themselves, it will be as if all of this — Mother and Father, Arinna, his brothers, the farm, the livestock, the lord of the estate and the manor house up the road, the echoing stables, the emptied village farther on and the abandoned settlements beyond that, all the way to the sea — as if none of it had ever existed. Unless he manages to find Arinna and bring her home. If he can't, there's nothing left here for him to come home to anyway.

Once at a harvest festival, the village priest grabbed Hani roughly by the upper arm and rang a brass bell in his ears.

"Hear that?" he told him. "Think you can tell when it's stopped ringing? You can't, can you? You know it's still ringing even when you can't hear it anymore. That's what your prayers sound like to the gods."

The priest was a drunk with a dog's eyes and a fawn's

heart, and nobody expected to understand the things he said, but Hani thinks about him now as he sits in the empty farmhouse. He can't help feeling that the stone walls are still ringing with the voices of all those who have vanished; he could probably hear them if his ears were as good as a dog's. All those people, there were so many of them, and they were so loud, and so laughing, and so scolding, they bellowed with pain or outrage, and sobbed, and mewled, and argued and barked for so long. Father and the boys were never quiet unless they were asleep, and even then they snored like bears. Arinna sang from morning to night, and her song found its way into every ear and every crack in the masonry. With all the noise they made, they must have left some sort of a trace of themselves, even a tiny one. Hani turns his head and plants his ear against the chimney stone, but he hears nothing. It's not the stone but his head that's still ringing with their voices, and that will go on ringing forever, he supposes.

If he lives forever, which who does? And when his head stops ringing after he dies, as it's bound to do, all those voices will be lost forever—Father growling and snapping at everyone, for any reason or no reason; Mother humming as she sews or rocks the babies to sleep or chops vegetables on the hearth; Huzzi and Arnu snickering and plotting, or sniveling after a thrashing; Arinna singing songs to herself that only she knows the words to; Zizi laughing at everything and everyone; Hushoo wheezing or barking in his sleep. It will be as if none of them ever lived because Hani will be the last one to remember them. The only reason we remember some people who lived long ago, he thinks, is because other people tell stories about them. If we stopped telling stories about them, no one would remember them either. That's what happens to most people, and it happens to all of Hani's people because no one tells stories about farmers and children, and everyone Hani has ever met is a farmer or a child, or maybe a miller or a horse-breaker, but it comes to the same thing. When they die, and when the people who knew them die, they're as forgotten as if they'd never been born. That's the way it is — it's what the priest and the pious call *fate*, and you can't do anything about it. Hani has never seen anything in this world to persuade him that fate is a real thing, and he wouldn't do anything about it even if he could, because he's only eleven and hasn't had a chance yet to do anything worth remembering, nor does he ever expect or care to, unless you count his knucklebones triumphs. Nobody he knows has ever done anything worth remembering, either. If they had, he'd remember. Hani knows how young and green he is, but he has seen how rock-stupid most grown-ups are and how little they're able to profit from their age and experience, and he's not impressed. Why anybody would want to be remembered for being too dumb to get out of their own way is beyond him. He retrieves five knucklebones from the pouch hanging on his belt and plays jump-the-ditch with half a mind while pursuing this line of thought.

A lot of people just can't bear the idea that no one will remember them. Hani is old enough to recall when the farm was teeming with grown men, and how, at harvest time and on feast days, they would gather around the fire in large, blustering groups and tell stories of violence and war, of epic voyages across the seas in pursuit of riches, glory, and honor, of men whose fame would never die because they had been brave warriors favored by the gods. And when these farmhands got into fights, as they always ended up doing on a bellyful of wine, they would insult and taunt one another with long-winded boasts of their own bloodlines and adventures, as if they, too, were glorious champions from a time when men were not so puny as they are nowadays. When he was little, Hani never understood what these grown men found so fascinating about it all, the ancient deeds and the insults and the violence, when none of them had ever traveled farther than a half day's cart ride from the cottage they were born in, when they all lived exactly the same lives and died exactly the same deaths. People are always saying that every person is different and unique, but nobody really believes it. Men like Father—and they're all like Father—like to see themselves as stallions or bulls, proud and alone at the center of their herd, but in their hearts they know full well they're all as exactly alike as heifers down the generations, no matter how hard they try to pretend otherwise. There's only one way to come into this world and only one way to live in it, as far as they're concerned, so the most they can hope for is to be allowed to choose how they're going to die. They never have a whole lot of imagination for that, either.

Hani returns the knucklebones to their pouch, then turns toward the hearth and pinches a frog's leg between his thumb and forefinger. It's just about done. He lifts the cattail, now charred, from the hearth and gently lowers the legs onto a rush mat on the plinth. Once they've cooled, he'll pack them in straw to mask their scent from hungry prowlers, wrap them in an oiled cloth, and add them to the other necessities in the rucksack. They won't last long, given the hardships of the journey ahead. One problem with catching frogs in the spring is that they're skinny, compared to fall frogs, so you need more of them. But the real problem is having to rely on frog legs to feed yourself in the first place.

Even when a farm is well run and the soil is rich and the climate fair, there's not a lot to eat in the spring. But Hani's farm, like all the farms of the valley, has barely had any able-bodied workers for several seasons, let alone managers and overseers, so the pickings have been slimmer still. No wheat was planted last year, and none will be planted this year. Any cattle or swine that weren't rustled in last summer's raids were salted and eaten over the winter. The goats turned feral and disappeared into the mountains, and the few remaining sheep will follow them soon enough. The vineyards have been untended for years and have reverted to the wild, while there's barely a fig or olive tree left standing from here to Mount Hazzi. And even if there were any seed left to sow, every last plow and axe was hauled away for the war effort long ago. The only crop the estate continues to produce is the winter barley, and Father took every last grain of that with him to market when he disappeared three weeks ago. And as for the stables — once famous throughout the empire for producing the best Nisean stallions in the land — they're no longer fit to house a rat, let alone a horse.

So Hani is reduced to frog legs, stale bread, and beer. There are still some of last year's beans and lentils in the storehouse, but with the kettle gone he has nothing to cook them in. He could probably manage to slaughter and butcher a sheep by himself, but what would be the point? He can't very well carry all that meat on his back where he's going, and even if he loaded it all into Ansa's panniers he'd just be making her a juicy target for every half-starved wolf or leopard within ten leagues. In any case, although he's never been to the city himself, he's pretty sure it can't be more than a three- or four-day walk from here. Five at most. If he runs out of food on the way, it won't be the first time he's gone hungry for a couple of days. And once he makes it to the city, he can surely earn his keep by picking up some manual labor. He reaches for a frog leg and nibbles at it.

Growing up on a farm is the best. You learn how to do everything on a farm. Hani has no idea what city people know how to do, but it can't be as many things as farmers know. There's nothing a farm boy can't do. Hani tries to imagine what the city will be like, what its people are like, but it's all muddled, fluid pictures in his mind that dissolve and flow away whenever he tries to focus on them. He has a vague memory of having once been told that it sits on top of a hill overlooking a vast plain that slopes down to a raging, endless sea at the edge of the world. His friend Tudha says that city people are blind and have white hands like mole paws, but Tudha has never been to the city and has no idea what he's talking about. Someone who had been there in real life once told Hani that the houses were so close to each other that there was nothing but narrow gaps between them, like gullies or ravines where the sun shines only at noon, but when Hani tries to imagine what that would be like, he keeps seeing these canyons as rivers, and the city people as fish. He knows that can't be right but he still can't figure out the correct way of imagining them. Someone else once said the city walls were twenty cubits high and ten thick, and that people lived on top of each other in buildings where your ceiling is someone else's floor, like honeycombs in a beehive. Hani has been to the mountains and seen trees that were at least twenty cubits tall and maybe more, and he knows perfectly well that no one could ever build a rampart as high as that. And as for the beehive people, that's plainly just an out-and-out lie. So he has only a very confused idea of the dangers ahead and of what is waiting for him there, and he knows that he will have to make a special effort to keep his cool and not allow himself to be flustered, because he's going to be more than frightened enough already, all alone on the road except for the donkey, without throwing dreamed-up terrors into the mix. The one thing he has heard from more trustworthy sources, and which he can well believe, is that the people of the city are so plentiful that they cannot be counted, like the fish in the sea or grains of wheat in a basket, and that they run around from morning till night doing all sorts of unimaginable things, and that more wealth and more wonders are to be found within its walls than anyone could hope to measure in one lifetime. More than anything, Hani looks forward to seeing all that gold and all those jewels for himself, but he's also concerned that his father and Arinna will be hard to find among the crowds, as rowdy as a flock of geese on the wing. And then, as if that weren't discouraging enough, there will also be the war to contend with.

Like all the children his age, Hani has never lived in a world at peace. He has been told that the first rumblings of war began the year he was born, or soon afterward. Nobody knows exactly when it started, because it was all so far away that it had been going on for ages before anybody in the valley was even aware of it. There were rumors of a fleet of invaders from across the sea, the mustering of troops and horses to the south, the drafting of blacksmiths, fletchers, armorers, and wheelwrights, but gossip like that was always circulating in this far-flung corner of the empire and it mostly couldn't be trusted. In any case, life in the valley remained unchanged long after the first stories began making the rounds. Even though Hani was a baby when the war started, he remembers his early childhood as one of plenty and ease. The valley and the river provided as generously as they'd always done—bumper crops of wheat, barley, grapes, olives, figs, and lentils, year upon year; pork, lamb, venison, and beef at every meal, or on every feast day anyway; bream, carp, and shad from the river, and sometimes even tuna from the sea. Every spring the valley's farms sent wagon trains groaning with fat bales of raw wool to be spun and woven in the city, and buyers came from all parts, speaking all sorts of exotic tongues and gesturing with their hands, to buy local thoroughbreds in a land where every valley had its own famous breeders and breakers. The land was rich in game, property rights were respected and sacred, and *family* meant generations living together under one roof. One of Hani's earliest memories, dating back maybe to when he was five, is of a funeral held for the chief's grandfather. The ceremonies had gone on for three days, and relatives, friends, and tenants had gathered from far and wide to mourn. What Hani remembers best were the three white steers, their curved horns gleaming with gold leaf, that were sacrificed on the makeshift altar, and the orgy of beef-eating that followed, the dark clouds of greasy smoke rising into the empty sky. Hani thinks that may have been the last time anyone in the valley ate so well without looking over their shoulder.

The sky is clearing, and a shaft of late-afternoon sunlight splits the gloom. Hani reaches into the rucksack for a loaf of bread. He rises and heads outdoors to take in the sunset, raising a jug of sour beer from the well before seating himself on the lip of the meadow that drops down to the river.

The changes came slowly, and many were not noticed by the children until the grown-ups started complaining about them or someone's father turned up missing, marched off one day for training in the local militia. Hani remembers one farmhand after the other boasting that he would never be drafted because his work was critical to the war effort, but very few were truly exempt because, like Hani's father, they were hereditary foremen, or because they knew the right administrators. In time, even the senior hands began to be picked off one by one, their disappearance confirmed when their children showed up to play one morning in floods of baffled tears. Those who remained took to griping bitterly at the end of the workday about the lack of manpower and the extra labor that came with it, until the day they themselves were dragged away to serve, and then no one ever heard them complain again. Little boys like Hani and Tudha and Alaksandu, who had always been considered too young to work in the fields, and even a few little girls were called up to fill in the gaps, but in the end they all proved too flighty to be useful and they were left to run wild again. The losses in grain, wine, meat, tools, and craftsmen mounted steadily, but every day there were fewer and fewer men left behind to moan about it and more and more caravans of destitute refugees, sometimes an entire village on the hoof, passing silent and haunted through the valley on their way eastward, who knew where?

Eventually, everyone in the valley, even the youngest among them, was forced to reckon with the growing shortfall of daily rations. Bread was still a fairly reliable staple but it was made with ever less wheat and ever more barley or chestnuts or even acorns. Red meat of any sort grew meager, then scarce, then disappeared altogether. Hani's valley was out of reach of the invaders' raiding parties, but villages that were closer to the theater of action were hit hard and took to attacking and plundering their own neighbors, even when they were connected by age-old clan ties. The forest communities stopped sending firewood and timber down the mountain, and before long fruit orchards and sacred groves that had been lovingly tended as long as anyone could remember were razed to the ground.

This far from the fighting, very little was known about the enemy, no matter how some people touted their so-called reliable sources. Even the fleeing refugees couldn't say what had hit them. Some claimed to have been informed that the invaders were called *Ahiya* or *Ahiyawa,* and that they had come from somewhere over the sea in a fleet of ships so numerous their masts made the harbor look like a forest. They had settled on the land like a plague of locusts, besieging the capital city and ravaging the hinterlands without pity. They were said to adorn their hair with grasshoppers and to speak a language that sounded like slugs feasting on wet lettuce. Some said they had come to liberate the land from its tyrant ruler and make its people free citizens; others said they wanted to enslave the local men and rape the local women because they were jealous of their virility and beauty; others still said that this entire country was once the invaders' homeland and that they had returned to assert their god-given right to it. There were even a few who claimed that the prince of the city had abducted the enemy queen and that the invaders had come to avenge the insult and take her home. The very idea of that made everyone laugh, but in their hearts they mostly agreed that it was the likeliest explanation by far. Even Hani knew better than to put much stock in these stories, but like everyone else he didn't know what or who to believe.

But the one rumor that everyone was able to agree must be true was that the enemy had a secret weapon in its ranks known as the Akhillisa. No one was quite able to say just what the Akhillisa was, exactly. If it was a man, the Akhillisa was more terrible and more bloodthirsty than any man ever born of woman. If a god, a demon exiled from all other gods. If an animal, one that had been starved in infancy and trained to prize human flesh above all others. Let loose among them, he — or it — could do more damage in one hour on the battlefield than an entire battalion in a day of fighting. Even the most seasoned and noble warriors risked their hard-won reputations by refusing to meet the Akhillisa in combat, skulking at the rear of a charge if there was any danger of an encounter with the creature. In any case, that was what the men said when they met around the beer cask. If valiant, battle-hardened knights refused to confront the Akhillisa, they said, what chance did a ragged mob of farmhands have, with their scythes and sickles? The men of Hani's valley were not known for being soft-spoken or moderate in their speech, but when they spoke of the Akhillisa among themselves they spoke in whispers. When rumors went around that the war was going badly, stories about the monster ran riot. When it was said to be going well, with victory in sight, tales of the beast's death were welcomed and shared with pathetic conviction.

Hani remembers the first time he heard about the Akhillisa very well, because it happened soon after Zizi drowned in the river. No one has ever accused Hani of being responsible for Zizi's death or even hinted at it; he was all the way on the far side of the farm when it happened and had not been tasked with minding his brother that day. But Zizi had been his special delight, his little pet brother who followed him everywhere and adored him, so he still blamed himself for what happened. Huzzi and Arnu were the big boys, too old and too busy to be interested in a toddler, and Mother was preoccupied with Arinna, who was a baby then, her first and only daughter, so once Zizi was able to walk Hani had taken him under his wing. They were inseparable; Zizi copied everything Hani did and made it very clear that he thought Hani was some sort of god. At some point, Hani had to stop doing certain things he loved to do when Zizi was around, like tree-climbing and slingshot practice, because Zizi would want to do them too, and Zizi would grow puffed up like a bullfrog and red-faced with outrage when Hani said no. Zizi was easy to love. The entire community adored him, even when he was on a tear. Unlike everyone else in the valley, he had light hair and blue eyes, which Mother used to say were as big as Ansa the donkey's, and he laughed a lot. Hani had seen how the youngest child in a family always laughs more than the others, and Zizi kept right on laughing even after Arinna was born because he refused to recognize her as a human being. There was a lot less laughter in the house after Zizi drowned, and not just because Zizi wasn't around to make noise.

The sun is setting now in the direction of the war and its monsters, somewhere out there across the rolling hills. The songbirds and waterfowl are mostly gone, but enough wildlife remains — frogs, bats, and crickets, but also some owls, swallows, and doves that have taken up residence in abandoned barns and cotes — to set up a decent twilight chorus. There's a faint scent of cherry blossom on the warm breeze, but it must be coming from somewhere very far away because all the cherry trees in the valley were chopped down years ago.

Hani has had his fill of bread and beer and sets aside his desire for food and drink. He stretches out on his back and awaits the appearance of the first star.

It feels like months since he stood on this very rise watching Father, Arinna, and Hushoo disappear over the hills at the head of a small caravan of carts and laden donkeys, but it was only three weeks ago. In the days before things got bad there were buyers for the farm's crops in every market town, but all those customers vanished long ago, so every year Father has had to travel farther and farther to sell his crops. He always used to take Huzzi or Arnu with him, or both when the harvest was bountiful, so once his brothers had gone off to the war Hani assumed that it was his turn to go, but Father wouldn't have it.

"What use are you to me?" he told Hani as he loaded the last of the donkeys. "You'd only cry and whine the whole way there and back. Stay here and tend to the sheep."

Hani would have begged to be taken along, but he knew full well that Father would never be able to tolerate his company for that long. Instead, he had argued for Father to leave Arinna and the dog at home in his care, but Father could not be persuaded, even by Arinna's tears. Father was well aware that he was walking straight into the teeth of the war, but he still felt that Arinna would be safer with him than in the charge of a softhearted, daydreaming, eleven-year-old misfit like Hani, at the mercy of every passing mercenary, vagrant, or man-eater, as he put it.

It should have taken them no more than seven days to get to the city, do their business, and return home. There are any number of reasons why they might be delayed, maybe even some happy ones, but there is so much work to be done on the farm at this time of year that nothing but an emergency, or worse, would prevent Father from rushing back as soon as he possibly could. Hani has little hope that Arinna's songs, as magical as they are, are powerful enough to keep them safe from the dangers of a city at war. He had held out hope of their return until three or four days ago, and had finally been forced to accept that they were not coming home. Father can take care of himself, or not, but there's only one person on the face of this earth who is destined to keep Arinna safe.

Everyone who knows Hani thinks he's a mouse because he doesn't like hurting things, and because his brothers and his father tell everyone what a little baby he is, and maybe they're right about him. He does not think of himself as a brave boy, not more than anyone else and surely less so than his brothers, but Arinna needs him and that makes him feel that courage is not what's required here, which is a good thing, as he's pretty short on courage and a little dizzy with fear. What this mission calls for is loyalty and pluck, and he has plenty of each and no mistake.

It fell to Arinna to take Zizi's place after he died, but they could not be more different. Zizi was bold and loud and fearless. Arinna is quiet and watchful and doesn't care what people think of her. She knows what happened to Zizi and she is more cautious than he was, more deliberate, but when she wants to take charge of a situation she can do it without saying a word. Although it's Hani's job to look after her, she's the stronger one and she always knows when it's time for him to stop taking care of her and for her to start taking care of him.

As far as Hani is concerned, he could never love her more than she deserves if he lived a thousand years and did nothing but spend all day every day telling her all the things she is to him. Sometimes he wonders if he's betraying Zizi by treating Arinna with such tenderness, but often when they are together he forgets which one he's with. It's almost as if Zizi can talk to him through Arinna. Zizi was all strut and bluster when he was alive, and he didn't have much use for careful listening, but now that he's dead Hani wonders if maybe Zizi has learned to speak their secret language, because it's a gift from a god that does not speak the language of the living. It's a gift to those who know how to listen for meanings that are too big or too distant for words to contain, and in death Zizi, like the gods, has grown very big and very distant.

And it's different too in another way, because when Zizi was alive there were still a lot of grown-ups around, not just Mother and Father, but also uncles and aunts and older folks who doted on him and needed his attention, and sometimes even tried to lure him away from Hani. Arinna doesn't need attention the way Zizi did, except Hani's, and in any case there has been a lot less attention to go around since Zizi died, and then Mother after him. But by the time Arinna was three or four most of those older folk were gone, too, either to the war or away from the war or in childbirth, so Hani has pretty much had her all to himself for the past few years. It's true she protects him with her songs and shares secrets in their secret language that she doesn't share with anyone else, but she also depends on him for so many things in a way that Zizi never did, and he feels not only that he has to teach her basic skills in a way that he did not have to teach Zizi, but also that he has to protect her in a way that he did not have to protect Zizi, because every day the world is becoming a more dangerous place for a little girl, even one with magic songs.

Some people are easier to imagine dead than others. Huzzi and Arnu, for instance, are boastful and reckless and a little dim. They barely seemed to notice it when Arinna was born or when Zizi died. They are close in age and very competitive with each other, like young roosters in a cockfight. They like to hurt things, especially Hani and his things. There was the time when Hani's pet goose Kurush died and he built a funeral pyre for her, and said prayers and spilled wine and even cut off a lock of his own hair to burn with her, but then Huzzi and Arnu snatched her off the fire and ate her. Only last year, Huzzi stole a gander from a neighboring farm, and Father forced him to return it and apologize. But then Huzzi demanded Arnu's cockerel as compensation for his loss, because he was the older brother and he was offended and humiliated to be without a fowl of his own.

Arnu refused and they came to blows, and when Arnu lost, as he usually did, he stormed off in a huff and refused to help bring in the winter barley. The crop was almost lost until Huzzi restored Arnu's cockerel. Hani has no trouble imagining that his brothers are dead. In fact, he would be surprised if they were still alive three days after they joined the army. The valley used to be crawling with boys like them. It's almost as if there's a fresh new crop of stupid boys every year, and that they are scythed down in their green age like spring wheat because that is what they are made for and good at, no matter what anyone says about young men being the wealth of a nation.

Mothers are pretty easy to imagine dead, too, mostly because there are so many dead mothers that no one needs to imagine them. Dead mothers are more common in the valley than dead sheep in the lambing season. Hani himself, as young as he is, has already seen a few dead mothers besides his own. Generally speaking, they all look alike once they're dead, especially here in the valley where most people look like each other anyway, unless their bodies or their faces have been damaged in some way, which is also not so unusual, given the many violent ways in which women can die and do die. Men die violently, too, but not in the quiet way that women do. There's hardly ever a fuss or a scandal when a woman dies in a domestic accident, especially here in the valley, where men are forced to marry their brothers' widows.

As for dead babies, well, they're just everywhere, more

numerous than the living and quieter, too. They are like old folk who fall asleep in the middle of the day, wake up in a daze for a few minutes, take a quick look around, then fall back to sleep. Dead babies have no idea what has just happened to them. When Zizi died, it must have taken him days to realize he was dead, and he would have been outraged when he figured it out. Knowing Zizi, on the other hand, he probably never did figure it out.

Dead fathers are a little harder to imagine. There aren't so many of them around, for one thing. Hani has never seen one, unless you count dead grandfathers, who are technically also dead fathers. They often go away to die, either because they're fighting somewhere or because they wander off in search of oracles and miracle cures when they're sick. It's true that men are much more afraid of dying than women, and ashamed, as if it were a weakness or a character flaw, so they'll often hide it until the last minute if they can. As a result, you don't see them lying around so much, hoping to be waited on or pitied. That's why it's so hard for Hani to imagine Father dead—almost no one else has a father who's still alive and working the land. When you ask him why he's still here when everyone else is dead, he just says that someone has to stay home and feed the children, which is fair enough but doesn't explain why it has to be him.

Hani has a hard time imagining himself dead, too. He has heard people describe the underworld and it does not sound like the kind of place he would enjoy. What would it be like to go from being alive one moment to dead the next? Is it like walking into a tree or like walking into the shade? It's one thing to look at a corpse and assume it's not feeling or thinking anything; it's another thing to imagine yourself as that corpse, because suddenly you're convinced that there must be something going on in there, some sort of deep sleep or dream. And even when they chuck you on the funeral pyre, you can't help picturing yourself floating up on a swirl of smoke, watching it all and thinking all sorts of things that you never could have thought when you were alive. If you close your eyes and try really hard to imagine yourself as a dead body you may convince yourself that you're doing it, but the truth is no matter how hard you try your mind won't let you believe that the world goes on without you after you're gone. It can't go there because it's not made to go there. Hani once accompanied his father to the mountains to talk with the woodsmen who lived there, and who had a kind of cart for hauling logs that had long, polished poles instead of wheels, for gliding over the snow. If you asked that cart to imagine itself gliding over dirt or grass, it just wouldn't be able to do it, because it was built for snow; it had a snow-mind and a snow-body that could never even imagine a grass-mind or a grass-body. It wouldn't even understand what you were talking about if you tried to explain how a wheel worked. Hani thinks that people have life-minds and life-bodies, and even though they have seen dead minds and dead bodies, in their hearts they don't really believe in what they're seeing. It's easier to invent gods in their palaces and underworlds than it is to picture a world that exists without you in it. Hani has tried, he tries often, but it's no use. He can only believe in what he sees and understand what he has experienced. He's seen plenty of dead people but he's never seen a dead Hani. Hani is a cart, not a sled.

By noon, Hani and Ansa are as far from home as they have ever been. Hani would have been even farther along if he'd left Ansa behind and taken the skiff, as the river is in flood and the city, they say, is directly downstream from the valley, but he feels like he would have been vulnerable on the river, easy to see from far away and with nowhere to hide. He also would have been lonely and even more scared than he already is if he'd been by himself. In any case, the road hugs the river all the way to the city—at least Hani is pretty sure it does, because this is the road everyone takes before they don't come back—and it's easy walking because there are few travelers to churn it into sucking mud, which is its usual condition at this time of year. And if someone comes along who looks like he would be best avoided, Hani and Ansa can just slink off into the woods or the underbrush until he has passed by.

But as it turns out, there are no woods or underbrush. As they make their slow but steady way toward the war, Hani is surprised to find that this new valley is more wrecked than his own. The next is likely to be even worse still. Back at home, most of the trees have been chopped down and many houses are in need of serious repair, but even so some livestock remain, a few fields have been plowed in preparation for sowing, and most farms are still managing to get some sort of barebones crew together for the spring planting. Just two or three planting seasons ago, the valley that Hani is passing through now would have been crawling with farmers, oxen, and mules at this time of year.

This is supposed to be the season of hope and rebirth, when everyone is hard at work helping nature wake up from her long sleep. Instead, anyone can see that the fields were not sown last fall or spring, and maybe for an entire year before that. Even now, in early spring, they're overgrown with thistle, mullein, and clover and most likely could not be turned over even if teams and plowmen were on hand to do it. Other than a lone boatman glimpsed easing his raft into the bulrushes shortly after dawn, Hani has not seen a single human being since he left home yesterday. Nor has he heard the thud of an axe, the whistle of a shepherd, or the call of a cattleman. No birdsong, no lowing herd, no barking dog, no cackling barnyard fowl, no pawing horse. The only sounds he has heard since rising this morning are his own footfall, the dull tread and snorting breath of Ansa at his side, the sigh of the breeze in the rushes, and the stream gurgling like a suckling baby.

The orphaned buildings strung out along the road and those set farther back in clusters below what used to be the tree line are long abandoned. Many have lost their doors, probably pulled off their hinges and broken up for firewood. Most have collapsed or collapsing roofs, their rafters and tiles pilfered, and not a few have clearly been put to the torch for the sheer fun of it. Here, a stone granary has been ransacked and lies sprawled on its side, as if pushed over by a giant hand. There, a wrecked mill squats, disintegrating over the stream that once powered it. Everywhere, the furrows choke on weeds and the farmhouses gaze empty-eyed over delinquent fields and terraces, like parents who have been disappointed by their children once too often and no longer dare to hope that they will amount to anything.

Hani and Ansa have met no one on the road, alive or dead. Whatever violence occurred here scared its victims away before it descended upon their homes. Maybe it was done to them; maybe they did it to themselves. There's no way of knowing. In the early days of the war, whole communities uprooted themselves and fled to the safety of the forests. The refugees who passed through the valley could tell you where they came from — usually, a village that no longer existed — but had no idea where they were going. The forests are long gone from the farming lowlands, so whoever lived here not so long ago is either dead or hiding in the mountains.

There's a difference between hearing rumors of a distant war and seeing with your own eyes villages and farms that were just like your own only a short time ago and are now laid to waste. The outlines of the streets are all there, as are the footprints of the homes and farm buildings that were swept away by whatever storm blew through here, but all life has fled. Like a fresh corpse that can sense that something important has just happened to it but can't quite manage to remember what it was, these ruined villages look as if they're dreaming that they're still alive and might wake up at any instant. But that instant is long past for these places. This is a dream they won't wake up from.

Ansa raises her head and shakes it, making her ears crack like whips. Hani could have ridden her all this way if he'd wanted to. She's carrying just the lightest burden of a blanket, a small sack of barley groats, and two waterskins, and she could easily have borne his weight. She has carried far heavier loads without complaint and has sometimes been used cruelly while doing it. If Father were here, he would insist that Hani ride and he would berate him furiously for sparing her. But Hani has brought her along more as a companion than as a pack animal. She's better company than Hushoo and is always steady in a crisis. He trusts her advice more than he trusts Father's or his own, and he can always rely on her sense of humor when he's feeling low or confused. She's a favorite of Arinna's, too, and will feel grateful to have been asked to participate in her rescue. It's an easy thing to reward her devotion.

In their first few hours on the road, Hani chatted amiably with Ansa in his normal voice, but his commentary has gradually been reduced to a hesitant whisper.

To pass the time, he tells her the old story about the time the governor sent an envoy, all perfumed and decked out in a wedge-shaped headdress and polished beads in his beard, on a fruitless errand to seduce the valley folk to barter their meager treasure for something he called "civilization." Ansa has heard this story before and she does not appear any more impressed by it at this telling than she did at the last. Her pace continues slow and plodding; her backside sways to its own rhythm; her head bobs as if she is silently singing a song to herself. She gives no sign that she has been listening to him, but Hani knows she has. He knows that she has heard every word he has said and that she understands the story better than he does but is too embarrassed to have to explain it to him. Hani knows, because Grandfather Panku told him so, that the difference between animals and humans is that animals never eat more than they need, animals never shit where they sleep, and animals never speak unless they have something to say.

Grandfather had a very dim view of the human race, and of Hani's father and brothers especially, but Hani took his opinion as a high compliment to animals, and most of all to Ansa. He knows what she thinks about people who talk too much, because she's told him so, more than once, and he tries to remember whenever they are alone together to keep his words to a minimum because a man with his mouth always open is like a bucket with a hole in the bottom. He wants her to think well of him because she is so superior, wise and true, but sometimes he forgets and allows the words to trickle unchecked from the hole in his face. Ansa is not a priest or a king. She's just a donkey, and not necessarily a young one at that, but if Hani were in a corner with the Akhillisa standing between him and the door, he would choose to have Ansa at his side over any priest, king, or warrior you might care to mention. He turns to her and she raises her head to return his gaze, but she is giving nothing away. With Ansa, you always have to work for your instruction; she makes you lean all the way in to hear what she has to say.

The day is beginning to exhaust itself as the valley rises to a shallow pass and the road and the river diverge until the next bend. As they climb, the sun disappears below the bald crest of the hill. It will reappear when he reaches the top, but it's a useful reminder that they should begin to look for shelter for the night. It will be hard to find a secure stronghold against nocturnal predators, chiefly wolves, but as long as it has four walls and a doorway that can be barricaded with debris, they should be all right. None of the houses has a roof, but leopards will not venture this far from the mountains, so the lack of a roof shouldn't be a problem, and they certainly won't need one for protection against the weather. Hani will keep his flint knife and his sling handy just in case, and a tidy pile of rounded stones within reach. It's not safe for Ansa to stay outside overnight, as she would at home, but she'll have an hour or so to graze before sundown, and he has enough bread to share with her if she's still hungry after that.

He's trying not to think about Arinna or Father, or what might have happened to delay their return home. He has no imagination for it and wants none. Instead, he thinks about Ansa because she is there before him and she is beloved, too. Like his sister, she is modest and beautiful. Her eyes are as black as the obsidian mined in the mountains out east, her teeth as white and pure as ivory, her mane streaked and undulating like the grain of Mount Ida pine. She walks with the dignity of a village elder, never hesitating and never deigning to turn to look at what is behind her. Hani would never tell anyone that his two most cherished role models are a six-year-old girl and an aging donkey, but he knows in his heart that Ansa, like Arinna, is a profound and original thinker. This is not guesswork on his part but an important truth. He's glad that he decided to take Ansa along for this journey, and not just because she's good company. He's not used to being anywhere this far from someone he loves; it's unnatural and he doesn't like it. Ansa's presence takes the pressure off. Even in his private heart Hani has no problem with that. Everybody needs love. This has been explained to him over and over again, by his mother at her breast, by his aunt when Mother was gone, by Arinna when she placed herself under his protection, by Ansa as she counsels and educates him. Father doesn't talk about love, of course, but he did once tell Hani that a seed stuck in a crack in a dry rock can't sprout without rain.

What love is, exactly, what its use might be, why you should be jealous and protective of it, no one can quite seem to put their finger on, but you know it when you feel it, like sunshine on your skin when your eyes are closed, or when you're so deep underwater in the river that you can't feel the sun's heat yet it still guides you to the surface. And it's only when you feel it that you know you need it. It's so obvious to Hani, even in the midst of war and death, that love is what holds the world together; even a child knows it, a donkey knows it, a trapped frog knows it. Arinna knows it. It's what allows her to go to sleep at night confident that she will wake up in the morning, or wander off to war with Father knowing that Hani will come for her if she needs him. It's what makes her so beautiful he can't tell if it's something everybody can see or something only he can see. When you find something that secret, it feels as if it has been waiting there only for you, like a nest full of blackbird eggs.

Hani finds an abandoned farmstead and spends the remaining hours of daylight in target practice with his prized sling, whose cords of twisted wool he made with his own hands. On a low wall, he arranges an array of targets—shards of wood, broken pottery, an old shoe, anything he can find—knocks them all off from a distance of ten paces, without missing a single one, then sets them up again and starts over from fifteen paces. It isn't until he reaches twenty-five paces that he registers his first miss. When he's done, he carefully recovers all his shot, small round stones that his expert eye has picked out from the riverbed, and returns them to their lambskin pouch, which he wears on a belt of braided reed around his waist, next to the knucklebones.

Hani chooses a derelict shed, its roof long gone, as their shelter for the night. He climbs to the top of a wall to watch the sun set. As they seep into the seams of the world, the colors remind him of the oily sheen spread by cypress cones on the surface of a woodland pond. As the sun disappears it sucks its colors back into itself, as if it's saving them in a jar for the next time it needs them. But instead of fading they turn red and begin to pulse like embers in a forge, or the opened artery of a sacrificial heifer. Hani thinks it's the strangest and slowest sunset he's ever seen, until he realizes that it's no sunset. Something very big is burning just below the lip of the horizon. It must be very far away because there's no whiff of woodsmoke on the breeze. He watches it for some time, but once it becomes clear that the fire is not going to go out, he hops off the wall and prepares himself for sleep.

Hani had a really hard time falling asleep after Zizi died because he kept sinking into the dent Zizi left behind in the pallet they had shared at night. But once Arinna took Zizi's place, she and Hani would stay up whispering for hours. She didn't tickle or fart like Zizi did, and when she fell asleep she slept so quietly you could hardly hear her breathe. Her body was cool and relaxed beside him, but even in her sleep she could tell when Hani was distressed or had a bad dream, which happened often enough, and she would shift so that some part of her, a toe or a knee or a shoulder, came to rest against Hani to calm him down. Every so often Hani would wake to hear her humming under her breath, and he knew she was singing in her dreams or some god was teaching her the words to a hymn.

It was around that time that Mother first began threatening Huzzi and Arnu with all the things the Akhillisa would do to them if they didn't behave and shut up and go to sleep. She must have thought that Hani and Arinna couldn't hear her or were already asleep, but they weren't and they could. Arinna was hardly more than a baby who could barely walk, but she understood everything Mother said, or else she was just terrified by the tone of Mother's voice, which had become a little shrill since Zizi went away. The stories she told Huzzi and Arnu in that furious whisper—about how the Akhillisa prowled the valley at night looking for children to eat and wash down with beer for breakfast, and how sometimes the severed limbs and heads of its victims got stuck between its fangs and their dead, gaping mouths seemed to cry out for help when it opened its slobbering jaws — were usually enough to keep the older boys quiet for a short while, but every night Hani and Arinna clung shivering to each other for what felt like hours before they were able to fall asleep. Mother's lullabies sometimes helped, but after she fell sick she could never stay awake long enough to sing more than one or two, and later not even that. Hani tried to take over lullaby duties for himself and Arinna, but Arinna would have none of it.

"You sing like a beast," she'd whisper in bed, pinching his forearm, "and you've got the words all wrong. Let me do it."

So Arinna assumed the responsibility of singing them both to sleep. At first, she only sang Mother's old songs, but she only knew a handful because she'd always fallen asleep quickly whenever Mother sang. But now she needed more songs because it took her and Hani so long to fall asleep by themselves, so she started making them up. Her earliest songs were about people and animals and places that she and Hani both knew, but soon she grew tired of having to find new rhymes and stories all the time, so she began to sing nonsense verses that eventually gave way to complete gibberish.

"Mazu bazu mamolinu pil,
Ulikummi upelluri hirihibi liu."

"Stop it! It doesn't mean anything."

"It means something to someone."

"Who? Who does it mean something to?"

"It means something to the god who sang it to me."

"Shut up! A god didn't sing that to you."

"Yes she did. It's a secret language to protect children from monsters."

"So what does it mean, this secret language of yours?"

"I don't know yet. She only taught me the words."

So Arinna began to sing the songs that would protect the children from danger, and because Hani slept right next to her he soon began to feel safe at night. She would spoon him from behind, lacing her arms around his chest, and sing directly into his ear, so that Huzzi and Arnu couldn't hear and demand that she sing for them, too. Anyway, she told Hani, her songs wouldn't work on them because they had cruel hearts. Her songs would wrap themselves around Hani's head and face like the softest, thinnest veils of linen, making her and him invisible and unsmellable to all monsters and demons and drunks. The other children heard about her powers—Hani boasted about them, of course, just as anyone would, even though they were supposed to be a secret—and asked her to teach them the songs, but she explained that even she didn't know where they came from or what language she was singing in, so she couldn't, and in any case they only worked at night when she was already in bed. It was true at first that she didn't understand the words of the songs, but she and Hani worked really hard trying to understand what they meant and they finally figured them out and the songs became their secret language that nobody else could speak. The rest of it she just made up because she only wanted to sing for Hani, and for herself.

Hani lies on his back, staring up at the stars framed by the four walls of the shed. Ansa sleeps standing beside him. He tries to focus his attention on the steady rhythm of her breath to help him fall asleep, but everything sounds like a wolf or a robber tonight. They say donkeys will sleep lying down when they feel perfectly safe, but Hani has never seen Ansa sleep lying down, and she knows best. He tries to match his own breath to hers, but it won't go. He's not scared, hardly at all, but he wishes Arinna were here to sing to him anyway. He tries to hear her voice in his head, but it doesn't sound right because he's outdoors instead of under the blanket back home. He tries to hold a conversation with her in their secret language, but the secret language is like a prayer or a wish—it doesn't make any sense unless someone is listening to it—and Hani can't speak it as fluently as Arinna can. Finally, he replays in his mind the entire game of toad-in-the-hole that won him the village knucklebones championship two years earlier, with every play made by all six contenders, and that does the trick. He dreams about his mother. She's sitting on the flat rock that juts out of the river just above the bend at Kuzi's mill. Arinna is on her lap. She's only a baby, but Hani suspects that she is actually the goddess Hebat, because her smile is that of a kind protector. Mother is looking away, but Arinna turns and stares right at Hani when he emerges through the rushes on the riverbank, as if she has been expecting him, and she beckons him to swim to her. He does, and when he pulls himself onto the rock it's so warm that it immediately makes him drowsy, so he stretches out and puts his sleepy head on Arinna's lap, even as Mother rocks and cradles Arinna in her own. A light breeze lifts a fold of Mother's linen dress, and through it Hani can see to the far bank of the river, where the water-wheel of Kuzi's mill, which was damaged in a storm two years earlier, has been repaired and is serenely revolving.

The next morning, Hani and Ansa find the corpses. They are in the river. They *are* the river, filling its bed almost bank to bank. They have been caught up behind a fishing weir of rush matting stretched halfway across the stream. Those farthest from the trap still have room to spin lazily, some floating on their backs, others face down, their limbs pin-wheeling. Those out near the center of the current or at the far bank blunder against one another and begin to revolve faster as they're swept around the bottleneck and beyond the weir, eventually to bobble off around the next bend in the river. Those closer to the weir are compacted against it and one another, their limbs interlaced like sleeping children sharing a bed, some with their heads resting on the shoulders or thighs of those ahead, some partially submerged, some with their faces pressed against the matting like pinned wrestlers. They are in various stages of undress, and a few are entirely naked. There appear to be no young people among them; they are all children or old folk — they were once anyway, not long ago — and their bodies all bear traces of having been hacked at or sliced or stabbed, although the cold water has flushed their wounds. Their eyes are mostly shut and their cheeks are still pinkish, as if they have recently exerted themselves in feats of speed or stamina, so they were probably alive this time yesterday. The hovering insects that dance above the surface of the water, and the martins and swifts that swoop down to feed upon them, seem unaware of the intrusion. The river water ripples and sparkles gaily in the sunlight.

Death holds no mysteries for Ansa, and she soon turns her attention to the bright young mugwort flourishing on the riverbank, but Hani is not done looking yet. The dead all have stories to tell; he knows that both from hearsay and from experience. He has never yet met a corpse that did not have something that it considered urgent to communicate to him. Some do it more loudly and insistently than others, but they all do it to some extent or another. These dead in the river are too quiet. He can't hear a word they're saying or be certain that they are even trying to say anything at all. That would be unusual, if not frightening. It's as if they all have a shared secret that they're hoping to keep from him. He would wait them out, stare them down and shame it out of them, but their eyes are closed and he imagines they have more time on their hands than he does. If Arinna were here, he thinks she might try to sing to alert him to her presence, but the dead have their own way of looking at things and you can't take anything about them for granted. He's going to have to investigate further.

He forages among the reeds along the waterline until he finds the weir keeper's ash pole. Firmly anchoring his feet at the water's edge, he begins to prod and nudge the bodies toward the center of the river, starting with those farthest away, which he can barely reach. None of them is big enough to be Father, but several could be Arinna. He's soon able to detach an old lady from the pack and send her around the weir's anchor post and away downstream. The next two are boys, then a girl about Arinna's size, but she's face up, so he knows it's not her. The next body is face down, also about Arinna's height and with hair that may or may not be the right color or length, it's impossible to tell at this distance. The only way to know for sure is to turn it over, but there are several other bodies in the way. From the riverbank, he tries to use the pole to nudge them apart, but they are too intertwined and compacted against each other and the pole isn't sturdy enough. He wades into the water, arms outstretched, and reaches his fingers into the crevice between the collarbone of one corpse and the crotch of another. They're cold and springy, like the leather skin of a coracle, but also wet enough that his fingers keep slithering off. He pushes again, and his right hand slips and its knuckles bounce off the old man's scrotum, hard enough to make him double over in pain if he had been able to feel it. Hani closes his eyes, plunges his hands deeper into the gap between the bodies, and wrenches them apart. The old man spins away, breaking the logjam of several other bodies, including the one Hani is trying to identify, and it begins to float away. Unless he acts quickly, it will be gone before he's able to reach it. He holds his breath and plunges into the water, swimming beneath several intervening corpses until he's right below the one he needs to look at. He opens his eyes and finds himself staring directly into its face. It's not Arinna; in fact, it's a boy. His skin is not pink, as it had appeared in the direct sunlight, but speckled like the egg of a thrush. The boy's expression is serene but his mind is racing. Now that he has Hani's attention, he begins to speak, to plead like they all do. He wants to go home, he tells Hani, just there over the next rise, where Mama has a big bowl of barley porridge ready for his supper and his brothers are waiting for him to complete a team of leapfrog. They were all playing together only a minute ago; their team was winning and he's itching to get back to it. He's hungry and he's twitchy and he's sleepy all at the same time; like many kids his age he doesn't really know what he wants. Hani is sure that Zizi was exactly the same in the moments after he drowned. Hani whispers silently to the little boy, tells him that they are all waiting for him just around the next bend in the river, and then he sends him off with a gentle shove.

45

In the end, none of the bodies is Arinna, and Hani has freed every last one from the weir's clutches, sending them all downriver to watch over the restless little boy with mottled skin. Hani rests briefly on the riverbank, his forearms on his knees, chewing mugwort to ward off nightmares, until Ansa nudges him from behind with her warm snout and a puff of moist breath between the shoulder blades. They move on, and the road puts a little distance between them and the river.

All of the buildings in this valley are damaged to one degree or another. Most have been burned, and some are still smoldering. There are no crops in the ground, but someone has set fire to the fields anyway. As it rises and falls, the road snakes through settlements that, if they were intact and inhabited, would have been larger than any Hani has ever seen but now stink of smoke, blood, and fear. Everything that was once whole and useful—buildings of every sort, but also fences, wagons, forges, altars, wells, communal ovens—lies shattered. The assembly of corpses in the river has given him a confused imagination for what might have happened to Father and Arinna that becomes harder to ignore with every gutted village. He keeps seeing them as fish-people swimming, or drowning, in the deep river-streets of the city. Hani and Ansa both struggle to avert their eyes, as there is almost nowhere to rest them that does not cry out in its disgrace and sorrow. As they ask themselves whether there are any people left alive anywhere, he notices a distant column of smoke rising over the horizon directly ahead in the west, then realizes that he has been looking at it for some time without seeing it. It leans away from the north wind that always blows from the coast at this time of year, and at the top it opens out into a many-vented fan, like a begging hand. A little later, when they crest a hill, he sees that it is an entanglement of thinner columns of smoke converging.

Not long after that, they reach a patch of wildflowers shel-tered from the wind by a low berm by the riverbank. Hani has heard that wherever a god has lain down to make love, there grow crocus, clover, and hyacinth. This would seem to be such a place. He and Ansa eye the carpet of flowers with suspicion and disdain until Ansa decides that the only hon-orable thing to do in the circumstances is to eat them. Some people believe that there are more than a thousand gods liv-ing on Mount Hazzi, but Hani has not been won over by any of the arguments that have been presented to him over the years. It's not that he doesn't believe the gods exist, or that gods of some kind share the world with humans. It's just that nothing he has ever seen of the natural world can persuade him that they have the kind of powers they boast of having. Why would a god who has the power to harness the thunder-clouds and the lightning as weapons against his enemies use them to burn down Talmi's hayloft or wash away Aljasi's henhouse? Why would a deity who could choose any god-dess on Mount Hazzi or any nymph in the sea as his consort bother rolling around in the mud with a sullen milkmaid, like Kanza claimed happened to her while her husband was away at war? It makes no sense at all.

Hani usually keeps this opinion to himself because people don't like to be contradicted, especially stupid people who look at one thing and see something completely different. Once at the dinner table Hani happened to mention his suspicion that the gods might be insane or simpleminded, and his father knocked him to the floor, where his brothers emptied a bowl of pottage on his head. Discussing the incident in bed that night with Arinna, she tried to persuade him that Father had proved his point, but that didn't make much sense. In any case, it's always possible that he's wrong about the gods, so why take a chance by badmouthing them? Probably safer and smarter to drop the whole thing. Either way, nothing he has seen in the past two days has shaken his conviction that a god's real power, much like the king's, is his ability to inspire fear, and that if you take that fear away there isn't much left of the god or the king.

Hani thinks of himself as someone who knows less than anyone else about anything. He knows nothing about warfare, fighting, lords and dynasties, weapons, chariots, faraway places, foreign tribes and their languages, public speaking, trickery, prayers, and sacrifices. He probably knows less than the donkey, and he definitely knows less than his six-year-old sister. So if the gods' powers are real, why would they destroy the world, then choose him, Hani, the most ignorant person alive, to be the only survivor? It makes no sense. Why would they do something so stupid? The only possible answer is that they have no idea what they're doing and that they're really bad at doing it. Or that they have spared him for a reason. And if that reason is to save Arinna, that means she must be alive.

They say that even the gods are powerless to prevent something from happening if it's fated to happen, or to save someone who is fated to die. Even if you have no idea what people mean when they talk about fate, maybe you can't just wave it off if it's more powerful than the most powerful god on Hazzi? "It's my fate," they say. "It was fated to be." What they seem to be saying is that nothing on earth or in the heavens could have prevented it from happening, whether it was meeting the person you will love for the rest of your life, being killed in battle, or stubbing your toe on a rock in the road. When Zizi died and then Mother died, people blamed it on fate, as if fate were a disease you catch or a defect you're born with. That means that Zizi and Mother were always going to die, and that they were always going to die in exactly the way they died, and there was nothing, nothing at all, that anybody could do to stop it because they didn't know what was coming until it was too late. Hani, too, is fated to die in exactly the way he is going to die, maybe now, maybe tomorrow, maybe in fifty years, but he won't know his fate until it happens to him. In the meantime, though, he can do anything he wants, anything at all, because no matter what he does it will lead him straight to his fate.

Hani stands up and lifts his left foot off the ground, while Ansa watches. So here, now, he's completely free to choose whether to plant one foot in front of the other. But he could just as easily set it down next to the other foot or behind it, couldn't he? To test out this theory, he lowers his foot partway in each direction, and sure enough it feels as if he could choose any one he likes. But if you believe what they say about fate, no matter what choice he makes it's the one, and the only one, that he has to make because he has been fated to make it from the moment he was born, and maybe even before that. Whatever you do is what you are forced to do, and nothing you feel about it or know about it can change that. If Hani is fated to put his left foot in front of his right foot, then his right foot in front of his left, and then his left foot again, all the way to the great city burning on the horizon, and there to find his sister, or not to find her, that is what he has to do, no matter how afraid he might be or how much he doubts that there's anyone left alive in the world to rescue. On the other hand, it doesn't matter how much he loves his sister, or that she could be stuck in a hole somewhere calling his name, or hurt or captured by the Akhillisa, or that he may be perfectly willing and happy to lay down his own life to save her — if he puts his left foot behind his right, then his right foot behind his left, and so on all the way back home, that is what he's fated to do. He can keep going forward or he can chicken out and go home — whatever he does is what he's meant to do, and no one can blame him for it, not Father, not Arinna, not Ansa—not even himself.

A war breaks out because the barbarians are fated to invade. The king summons his greatest lords and advisors and tells them to prepare to fight. The lords go to their own dominions and order their chieftains to raise an army. The chieftains call up their knights, and the knights raise levies of commoners. The commoners go off to fight, leaving their wives and children at home. All of it, every last little bit of it, is fated to happen exactly the way it happens, and at the very bottom, at the lowest point you can reach in this chain of destiny, is him, Hani. It wasn't always like that, he knows, because he has heard stories of the golden age when mortal humans were like gods, when you didn't need to break your back and waste your strength plowing and sowing the land if you wanted to eat, and when no one bossed anyone else around or made them do things they didn't want to do. But if you follow this chain all the way from Hani, standing here on this berm by the river at this very moment, with death behind him and death ahead of him as he tries to figure out the right thing to do, the fated thing to do, all the way back to the days when no child was alone or scared or forced to make decisions he is completely unprepared to make, then it all begins to make a little more sense. If you follow it all the way back to the golden age, it all seems to lead—all of it, the gods, the earth that feeds us all, the wars and the kings, the farmers tending their fields, the woodsmen felling the forests, the houses going up and falling down, the babies being born and growing up and passing away, the dead brothers and mothers, the frogs and the fishing weirs — it all leads to this journey and this day and this berm. All of it happened exactly the way it had to happen just so that Hani would go off in search of Arinna, and nothing can change that. He has no choice in the matter. It's his fate.

By THE NEXT MORNING, the city on the horizon has burned itself out; just a weak smudge of brown haze lingers above it. Hani estimates that it's no more than three hours away, and Ansa agrees. The rolling hills and shallow valleys give way to flat fields, and the road straightens and diverges from the river, which meanders off on its way northward between low banks overgrown with flowering blackberry bramble and wild flax. Hani can see, even from this distance, that the city sits atop a hill that rises solitary from the plain, just as the stories say it does. They also say that it overlooks a broad bay that leads to the open sea, but there's no sign of water or hint of salt on the breeze, which is now blowing strong and hard from the north. The sun is more glaring here than it is at home and seems to sit higher in the sky, which has been purged of its violet by the wind.

Like most people he knows, Hani doesn't care to use place

names except when absolutely necessary, because they smack of the foreign and the unknown, and naming places brings bad luck. Everyone back home in the valley knows the name of the city, but they all just call it "the city." Very few places in the valley have permanent names. *Kurunta's farm* will be known as *Mursili's farm* after Kurunta dies and Mursili takes over. *Kuzi's mill* will be *Zidanta's mill* soon enough, maybe already is. The river has always been called the Sima, but everyone just says "the river." The valley itself doesn't have a name—unless you count "our valley"—and yet everybody knows exactly where to find it. Sometimes, some important place like Tarhuntassa's fortress will keep the name of the man who built it even after he's dead and gone, but there are almost no important places in the valley other than the fortress, and even that isn't very important. No one important ever goes there, and now it sits abandoned anyway. There are just a few market towns and no cities, but people know what a city is, more or less, and a few, like Father, have even been to one.

Everyone says that everything you need to learn about the world and other people, you can learn in your own valley, among people you know. You have to leave the valley and travel far beyond the places where people speak your language before you can expect to stumble on a city like the city on the hill, so places with names like Wilusa or Kanesh or Hattusa are alien simply because they have names, no matter what's in them or who lives there. In any case, no one in the valley has any clear idea of what's in them or who lives there. Even though the city is just a few days' walk from the valley, only Hani's father and one or two other local men had ever been there before the war. Now, most of them have been there, but none of them has come back to report on it.

As he approaches the city, the road is increasingly strewn with rubbish. Hani keeps his eyes alert for anything useful, but mostly it's broken junk that the former owners did not think worth saving: lengths of frayed rope, filthy rags, cracked jars and pots, soiled swaddling cloths, bloody bandages, the sole of a sandal worn down to a feathery leaf, a couple of hopelessly damaged wagon wheels, a few items that Hani is unable to identify. Here and there is something that, if he had found it near home, he might have considered scavenging for repair, but he can't afford to burden himself or Ansa with unnecessary cargo and he leaves it all untouched. All except an amulet of baked clay, about the size and shape of a duck egg, dangling from a snapped leather strap. He suspects that it has been lost rather than discarded. It's not especially pretty or well fashioned, but he's intrigued by the markings etched into all sides of its surface, like the scratchings of hens in the dust of a farmyard. He wonders if they hold some sort of magical power that could prove useful in a scrape if he can learn how to harness it. He's heard about this sort of thing. He's heard somewhere, maybe from the priest, that there are people who are able to communicate with each other over long distances using symbols or patterns that they scratch on a stone or a block of wood or something. It's not very clear in his mind and he's not sure how much he ought to let himself believe in such stories. Hani has never met anyone who knows how to do this magic, so he's naturally wary. Every so often tradesmen pass through the valley on their way from one faraway place to another, and they always leave some sort of tall tale behind for the farmers to sniff at, like a turd, but everyone says that most people from the outside are liars. Still, there's something about this story that has always fired Hani's imagination. It makes him think of his secret language with Arinna and all the things you can say in it that you can't say in ordinary talk. There's magic in that, too, but nobody except maybe Tudha and Alak would believe him if he told them, so he's kept it to himself all this time. Maybe the people who know how to use the symbols feel the same way.

Sometimes at night, he lies awake trying to imagine what these strange symbols would look like. What kind of symbol would there be for a frog, or a crane, or a donkey, or a boy? Are they pictures? If they are pictures, wouldn't it just be faster to say the words instead of drawing them? What would be the point, if it's harder to say or to understand than the thing itself? The people who know how to do these things, he's heard, are rich people, smart people, people who have been taught to do things that others don't know how to do. Why would they waste their time on something pointless? There has to be more to it, more than just silly old drawings. There must be something else, but he can't imagine what it would be. Hani looks at the world and he knows what he sees. As far as he can tell, the best way to understand the world is to look around and figure out how it works. You don't need drawings for that. If you know how to use your eyes and your ears, you don't need anything more than what your senses tell you. So he thinks the stories about the symbol people are probably just made up by other people who never learned to see the world the way their eyes were meant to show them.

But when he gets to the foot of the hill on which the city stands, he finds two stone columns on either side of the path that winds up the slope to a gate. The columns are square-sided, about his own height, and both are covered with more of the same scratchings like those on the amulet, so it must mean something important. Maybe this is the silent language, the brain language in which rich people are said to speak to one another? The column on his right also has a picture of a man in a tall hat, carrying an axe in one hand and a flail in the other; the column on his left shows a god with a lion's head driving a chariot. Hani raises his hand and runs his palm along the smooth, cool surface of the second column. The only drawings he has ever seen have been painted onto polished tree bark or flattened reeds with charcoal or crushed minerals mixed with glue, but these pictures have been cut directly into the stone so that no one can ever erase or change them. He can't even begin to imagine how this was done or who could have done such a thing. These things give Hani a new appreciation for the magic amulet in his rucksack.

He lifts his eyes and squints at the slope ahead and the stone ramparts at its summit. So the stories are true. The only time he has ever seen walls this tall and straight, they were cliffs in a river canyon in the mountains, but these cliffs are even taller than those and were built by humans. He can clearly see the crevices between the massive blocks, each as big as a hay wagon yet perfectly snug and aligned side by side and one on top of the other to a height higher than any building Hani has ever seen. He can only imagine how Arinna must have felt when she first saw them three weeks ago. She probably squealed like a piglet, as she does whenever she sees something new and thrilling for the first time. One of the best things about her is how easily she's thrilled by the world's endless surprises.

The path to the gate is narrow, steep and busy with switchbacks, okay for a man on foot or horseback, or for a mule train, but completely unsuited to a wheeled vehicle. Father and Arinna took the cart with them, so they won't have come this way, but Hani thinks that maybe he'll be able to see something useful from the top of the hill. As he climbs, he keeps his eyes on the walls and his hand on the sling; there must be someone up there watching him, even if he has seen no sign of life so far or heard so much as a cough or a fart. From this vantage point, he can see that there must still be some fires burning within the walls, and the air is heavy with the smell of charred wood and something harder to identify. Ansa is not happy and lets him know it. Near the top of the path, he stumbles on something hard and heavy— a real helmet made of shiny bronze! Another first for Hani. It's warm to the touch, and heavier than he had imagined, unadorned but intact except where the nosepiece has been staved in. It's an awesome find, worthy of being tried on, but when he rotates it in his hands it vomits a stream of sun-cooked blood onto his legs and feet. Hani drops the helmet; it clatters hollowly down the rocky slope and comes to rest at the bottom. Hani wipes at his legs and feet with the linen of his rucksack, to little effect.

Near the top, the path leads to an arched wooden bridge that crosses a deep trench cut directly into the bedrock around the entire walled perimeter, or at least the part of it that is visible from here, and ends at the foot of a great stone bastion into which the gate is set. The gate is taller than a hayloft and made of massive timber planks strapped and hinged in iron. It's ajar but only a crack, not enough for Hani to squeeze through, and it won't budge. At first, he thinks it's just too heavy for a boy to move, but then he realizes that there's something immovable blocking it from the other side, and when he presses his face to the gap he sees that what is blocking it is a twisty tangle of human corpses, piled one upon another almost to his own height. Some have managed to reach their arms through the gap as if they were trying to claw their way out, which is probably exactly what they were trying to do even though it was certainly hopeless even while they were alive. Their fingers are still hooked urgently onto the gate, and one such finger wears a heavy ring of gold and polished onyx. Hani exams it closely; clearly, the person who owned the hand that wears the ring never touched a plow in his life. Even in death, the hand is slim and elegant, its nails polished, and at this distance it smells faintly of lavender. The ring finger has withered enough for Hani to slip the ring off just like that. It will make a nice gift for Arinna when he finds her. He puts it into the pouch at his waist.

Hani heads north, following the strip of rocky brush that separates the foot of the rampart from the trench. He can see that this slope was heavily wooded not so long ago, but now it's stripped of all but the most stubborn scrub. The city walls sit upon the top of the hill like a crown, and as they curve westward the sea gradually comes into view. This is the first time in his life that Hani has ever seen the sea, but he knows what he's looking at because it has often been described to him and there's really nothing else it could be. He's disappointed to find himself less impressed than he'd hoped to be. It's leagues away, for one thing, at the far end of a broad, empty plain, and there is not as much water in it as he's been led to expect. It's a wide, bowl-shaped bay, partly enclosed by curving headlands, like jaws. It's more water than he's ever seen in one place, to be sure, but it hardly stretches as far as the eye can see, as he's been told it does, far from it. Still, it's a very pretty thing, to be sure. From this distance you can't see the waves moving, but they're lovely to look at as they sparkle in the sun and scuttle and bow before the wind just as young barley does. Ansa sneezes, as if she too finds it all a little less than amazing.

As the rampart begins to curve southward, it's interrupted by another, lower wall that sprouts from its base and stretches far down the hill, punctuated by towers. Here, too, there is a massive wooden gate set into a bastion, but it's locked tight. Hani believes that he might just be able to climb up the corner where the rampart and the lower wall meet, as they're both lightly canted, but he worries that if he leaves Ansa here it could be difficult or dangerous trying to get back to her once he finds himself on the other side of the wall. It may not be obvious to outsiders, but she depends on him for many things that she can't do for herself, and he takes that responsibility seriously.

They push on as the hill slopes gently downward. The wooden guardroom at the top of the next tower has been torched and is ready to topple, but the gate itself is sealed shut. Hani is in no hurry to see whatever new horror lies on the other side of the wall. He wonders if this is the way Father and Arinna came, or if they were admitted through one of the gates he has already passed. If they managed to complete their journey without delay, they should have gotten here more than two weeks ago — long before the city was set ablaze. They could have finished their business on their first day, within hours of reaching the city, really, then found that their return home was blocked for some reason and been forced to take a roundabout route back to the valley in order to skirt occupied territory, or even a ship up the straits to one of the port cities north of the valley. There were many ways they could have taken, but why would they have remained in the city long enough to be caught up in whatever it is that happened here?

They come to the charred ruins of a once-majestic oak, guarding a gap in the wall where another tower and gate once stood but which is now just a hillock of rubble and burnt timbers. The embers are still warm to the touch, and Hani wipes the charcoal off his fingertips on Ansa's flank. She reminds him to think of Arinna, as if he could be thinking of anything else, and to be brave, no matter how hard his heart pounds in his chest. They climb the mound, picking their way gingerly through the hot spots, and pause at the top.

So now he knows.

The entire city lies at their feet, sloping down to the lower walls and a gate tower to their right, inching up the hill to the ramparts of the citadel to their left. The mound they're standing on is not especially high, but still they can see everything. Directly ahead is a broad, curving lane, paved with smooth stone, that separates the upper town from the lower and intersects with another snaking up from the southern gate to the citadel. It's not the city of his imagination because he could never have imagined anything so vast and bewildering as this, not in a thousand years. It makes his imagination look feeble; it mocks words and thoughts and dreams and song. It's definitely not true that everything you need to learn about the world and other people, you can learn in your own valley, among people you know. This is not something Hani could ever have learned at home.

Before descending into the city, he rummages in his rucksack for the woolen shawl he has brought along to keep himself warm at night, and he wraps it around his head to cover his nose and mouth. Ansa appears to close her eyes as she finds her footing on the rubble. They move toward the heart of the city. There's no sound but the echo of the donkey's footfall against mud brick, and the occasional crackle and sigh of dying fires.

Like anyone raised on a farm, Hani knows death. He knows what it looks like and smells like, in the home, in the livestock pens, in the fields and the woods, in the river. It has never bothered him much, not since he was just a little kid at any rate, nor has he ever understood what people mean when they call a death "unnatural." Nothing, not even birth, is more natural than death, be it ever so violent. Sure, it has a way of insulting the eyes and the nostrils, but that goes away; in the end you can get used to anything. Strangers, friends, family—none of that matters a whole lot when you stop being afraid. Even Arinna—it's not so much the possibility that she's dead but the small chance that he might find her alive that moves him. That's the bargain that the living strike with one another, to help each other stay alive; you've got to honor it even when you know full well it's a lost cause.

These dead, like those he found in the river, are fresh as can be. Someone made them dead just now — not this morning, maybe, but probably yesterday and definitely not longer than two days ago. In Hani's experience, people who know they are about to die understand what has happened to them much faster than do those whom death has taken by surprise. He stops and listens in case any of them are still talking to themselves, but they all seem to have figured it out by now. He minds his steps so as not to alert them to his presence. They don't stink yet, except those that were incinerated as they cowered in a corner of their home while it burned to the ground. The blood that poured from the dying and the wounded and pooled around the drains set into the pavement is now the same dull brown as the mud bricks that most of the buildings here are built of. How strange to think of all the terror and confusion and noise that must have swept through this quiet place. Now it's almost peaceful, as if all these bodies that were humming with life and strength and desperate to stay alive so recently are grateful to have left all that behind them and at last take their rest in the bosom of death, as the priests call it.

But how they clung to life right up till their last moments! Virtually every body here died as it was running away, and they were all running in the same direction, probably trying to reach the ramparts of the citadel where they thought they would be safe from the people who did this to them. They all bear deep wounds from swords, knives, arrows, spears, in their heads, shoulders, backs, buttocks. Many have had their skulls bashed in with cobblestones pulled up from the paving. It was done in a hurry, too, as if they deserved no better and the killers had time only to do the bare minimum before moving on. No one here has been extravagantly disemboweled or mutilated in any way that would suggest they were hated by the people who killed them. It is odd, though, that almost every dead body here belonged to an old person. Where are all the children, the young women? There's barely a healthy-looking man, woman, or child among the dead. That sounds like a joke when Hani reruns it through his mind, and he almost laughs but then doesn't. And there are so many of them. Who would have thought that one place could have so many grannies and grandpas? There are more people here than Hani has ever seen in one place in his lifetime, even if they are all dead. If there are this many dead people in the city—and these are only the old folk—it's hard to imagine how crowded it must have been when they were all up and about. Maybe some of these dead were the enemy, but Hani is pretty sure most of them were locals. Winners bury their dead or incinerate them. Losers don't bury themselves, as a rule.

As they push on, Hani is very much aware of the dark alleys that branch off to the left and right and disappear into the bowels of the city. These lanes, he imagines, are where the people lived, where the homes are. They're also where someone who was trying to escape the slaughter might have succeeded in hiding. Flint blade in hand, he tries his luck down one of the alleys, only to find that every house has been torched, nothing left but brick walls holding each other up—brick walls and the charred bodies propped up within them, teeth grinning in the gloom. If Arinna and Father sought refuge in there, they are now lost forever. In his mind, Hani sings to himself the secret song that Arinna sings to him when he's afraid of ghosts in the night.

Here on the main street is the marketplace where those people used to come for food and other necessities. There are no shopkeepers in Hani's valley, but he's been to market towns before and recognizes the stands where vendors display their wares. They've all been smashed and ransacked, but there's still merchandise left where it fell—fruit, vegetables, bread, cheese, pots that may have held wine or milk or oil. Here's the shop of someone who sold meat, his wares mingling with the butchered corpses at its threshold. There's a place that sold fish, which, scattered gape-mouthed on the pavement, are beginning to reek. The stalls of a sprawling stable barn are piled shoulder-high with discarded children's tunics, robes, and shoes. A modest temple squats desecrated by the bodies of the priests who were slaughtered on its altar. A well and watering trough are filled to the brim and overflowing with bodies. He passes a bakery, its loaves scattered across the roadway. He gathers a few for his rucksack; they're still soft and have been warmed by the sun, making them feel as if they're fresh from the oven. At a major crossroads, where those fleeing the lower district collided with those coming from the east and west, the dead are piled up to the height of a young fig tree. Hani does not think they could have done this to themselves. Someone must have moved them later, maybe to clear the road. For whom, or what? Hani clutches his sling. It would be funny if he had to kill the last person left alive on earth, besides himself and Arinna. He and Ansa turn toward the citadel.

The road begins to rise and skew. They cross another wide street, where the houses crowd right up to the foot of the citadel ramparts, and reach the ramp leading to the main gate. It's wide open. On the very threshold of the gate lies a helmet, bronze like the first one but stamped with eyebrows and furrows on the brow and bearing a crest fashioned like a horse's mane. It's not the sort of object that is easy to misplace. Hani kicks at it and it rolls over several times. There does not appear to be blood or anything else inside. He picks it up, turns it this way and that, tries it on. It's too big, but not so much that it bobbles on his head. The inner surface is lined with felt pads to cushion it against his scalp. He turns to Ansa for her opinion, but if she has one she is wise enough to keep it to herself.

Just inside the gate is a wide, sloping plaza surrounded by grand buildings with marble columns and porches. They have been torched like the rest, but enough of their sturdy walls remain upright to give a sense of how mighty and intimidating they must have been before the war. This is where all the men of fighting age are; their bodies have not been treated with the same restraint as those of the common people in the lower town. Hani guesses that these men were soldiers, and that their corpses were stripped of their armor and abused by the victors. They smell worse, too, because many have been eviscerated. Ansa closes her eyes again, snorts, and kicks at the cobbles beneath her feet.

At the center of the plaza is a large wooden platform on wheels, which have been chocked to prevent it from rolling downhill and out the gate. On the platform are four wooden posts or columns that have been styled to resemble the legs of a giant horse, broken off above the knees in front and below the hocks in the rear. The rest of the horse, if that's what it was, is gone, smashed, burned and intermingled with the shattered scrap strewn across the square. Hani and Ansa move on again, ever upward. Through the open doors of a huge temple, they see a golden statue of a woman, as towering as a tree. She wears a tall helmet on her head and holds a shield in her left hand and a spear in her right. She is completely undamaged and her bare skin glows like the dawn. Her outstretched arms are draped with women's gowns.

This is obviously where the rich people and the leaders used to live, maybe even the king himself. The streets are broad and walled; on either side elegant stairs lead up to more temples, statues, and colonnaded mansions, their doors ripped off or hanging askew on their hinges, the fountains in their interior courtyards still gurgling. Hani enters a few courtyards, looking for a water source that has not been contaminated with gore. Leaning over the rim of a low marble basin, he catches sight of his reflection in the water. The helmet conceals his face entirely within its inner shadows; even his eyes are invisible.

He wonders about the man who wore it. How did he lose it? Was he killed or did he set it aside while he was celebrating his victory? His head was in this very helmet only two days ago, his eyes looked out of these same eyeholes, his breath warmed the bronze right here where Hani's own mouth is now. His brain was exactly here, occupying this very space where Hani's own brain now sits. What language did it think in? What thoughts did it think? Are there any traces of its thoughts left in the helmet? Hani feels like if he concentrates hard enough he might be able to hear some of those thoughts, so he does but he can't. How many helmets are out there right now, buzzing with the thoughts of dead people in their own language, while their families, maybe thousands of leagues away, believe or hope they are still alive? Hani has seen hundreds of dead in just the past few hours—how many of them have left behind someone who remembers their name, who knows who they were and what they did and said and worried about, the way Hani knows Arinna? Not many, he imagines. Does it matter? When he looks at them, every face, even those of the grown men, is Arinna's. And when it isn't it still is, because it's the face of someone who must have been loved by someone else. And because that someone else may be here, among the dead, Hani suddenly feels that he's searching on their behalf, too. The dead belong to the dead and to the living; the living belong to the living and to the dead. He's not sure if that means anything, but his head is spinning. He removes the helmet and stares into its blank eyes, sets it down on the rim of the basin. He washes the caked blood off his legs and feet and moves on.

The top of the hill is crowned with the largest building of them all. If Hani had to guess, which he does, this would be where the king and his family lived. He tethers Ansa to a pillar and ventures inside. Much of the roofing has collapsed, forcing him to clamber over piles of charred beams and broken tiles, but the walls are still standing, mostly. If there are any bodies in here they are buried under the wreckage. The hallways go on forever and the chambers are big enough to house an entire village. It's anyone's guess what purpose all these rooms could have served. He eventually comes to a great hall with a table as long as a barn and benches up and down its long sides. White linen curtains, smoke-stained and singed at the hems yet somehow still billowing in the breeze, lead out to a terrace overlooking the bay, which lies far below the city like a prize.

One wall is decorated with all sorts of colors under a

coating of smut. Hani yanks one of the curtains off its rod and dabs at the greasy soot before him, revealing a picture of an archer in a chariot, his bow drawn as he prepares to release an arrow, while his driver clings to the reins. Their horse rears, but it's not clear if it's stomping or leaping over the fallen foot soldier beneath it. The picture is so lifelike Hani can almost hear the horse whinnying, the driver shouting, the fallen man screaming. Hani goes out to the fountain on the terrace and soaks the curtain in water, then proceeds to clean away the soot. He drags a bench to the wall and stands on his tiptoes, but he still can't reach the top, where the soot is thickest. By the time he's done, most of the wall has been uncovered, and he steps back to admire his handiwork. The picture is teeming and pulsing with hordes of people doing different things: soldiers in battle, priests slaying sacrificial animals, sailors rowing a galley, workers stacking pots, animal-headed gods weighing human souls (maybe), hunters chasing a leopard, a king and queen, bigger than the gods, receiving gifts from kneeling slaves. One of the slaves is a little girl who looks a lot like Arinna. There's even a farmer behind a plow pulled by an ox, very much resembling Father in his white loincloth. You could imagine that at night by torchlight, with the shadows of the curtains billowing across the wall, the figures might look as if they were being moved by the power of their own souls. Your own shadow might mistake them for real people and try to dance with them.

It's incredible, of all he has seen today the most astonishing.

Hani has never seen anything like this, he has no idea what to call it, but he understands what it means without having to think. People don't often use the word *beautiful* back in the valley, unless maybe about a young woman or an especially sturdy bullock, but that's what this is, he knows it without having to think about it even if he still doesn't quite understand what he's looking at. It's as if someone has corralled the whole world and everything that has ever happened in it and trapped it in clear amber at the very height of its pride and strength so that it will live forever and never grow old. Surrounded by death and silence, it glows and pants like a newborn baby. Hani thinks about how, when you dream, there are a thousand details that you hardly notice and don't remember when you wake up, but you know they were there. This image is what a dream would look like if you could freeze it and study each and every little scrap of it at your leisure. Arinna would squeal and squeal if she saw this. He wonders if the people who caused all the ruination here looked at it and felt like he does, and if they paused for even a minute to ask themselves what they were doing. He can't believe they hated beautiful things, since they did not destroy this painted wall like they destroyed everything else. And now it has survived the city itself, and with no one left to ruin it, it might last forever, for whoever comes next, if anyone comes next.

On his further explorations, he comes across a chamber that must have been a bedroom, where he finds a brocaded robe under a pile of fallen timber. When he shakes it out he finds that it's all but undamaged. It's made of shimmering colors and a kind of fabric he doesn't even know what it is. It's lined with brushed wool the color of eggplant and softer than anything he has ever felt, like a kitten's underbelly. He thinks it must have belonged to a queen, and decides that he will sleep in it tonight. Also concealed under the rubble, he finds a lady's brooch of polished green stone, carved with a hunting dog killing a fawn. He's inclined to leave it, as it is useless to him, but changes his mind and drops it into his rucksack. Farther on, he comes across a room lined floor to ceiling with baskets containing clay tablets, each the size of his palm and covered edge to edge in the same tiny, mystifying inscriptions as his amulet. He helps himself to one. On the lower level of the palace, he finds the kitchens, row upon row of ovens big enough to sleep in, and another room filled with blocks of ice swaddled in thick blankets of fir branches. Hani has seen ice before, on expeditions to the mountains, so he knows what it is but has no idea what use it could possibly serve. A stairway cut into the bedrock leads to a spring of fresh water deep underground. He kneels and drinks deeply, then fills the waterskin for Ansa.

She has not enjoyed being left alone for so long in a place like this and she is happy to see him. He waters her and they share a loaf of bread. She's limping a little, and he agrees with her suggestion that they should begin looking for somewhere to sleep for the night. Ansa is not one to express her feelings frivolously, but Hani believes that this day must have taken its toll on her and shaken whatever remained of her faith, as it has shaken his, that the world is something that can be understood. It's even harder to bear when you keep your feelings and thoughts to yourself, as he believes Ansa has been doing throughout their journey, because giving free rein to them would be dangerous and unnerving. Even a soul as great as Ansa's has its limits. He drapes his arm around her neck and buries his face in her coat, which smells of hay and home. He hears the slow tattoo of her heart and his head rises and falls with her breath, and he wishes more than anything that he could be more like her, strong and brave like her, or that she would agree to share more of her wisdom with him than she does, without making him have to work so hard for it. She readjusts her stance, as if she is considering his wish.

They decide not to spend the night within the city walls, convinced that the ruins are haunted by the restless ghosts of the slain. Hani can already hear them clearing their throats and rehearsing the stories and requests they intend to ply him with, but he has no patience for it today. He and Ansa make their way out of the citadel and through the lower town, exiting from the same collapsed gatehouse they had scrambled over to get in. Hani finds a wedge of timber that's still smoldering, and takes it with him in the hope of starting a fire with it, but outside the city walls there's no wood of any kind to be found. They follow the outer wall downhill until they reach the southern gate tower as the sun touches the rim of the low-slung hills that form the western ring of the bay. The gate itself is gone, but the gatehouse is undamaged. They head onward along a wagon trail that leads from the city down to a ford in the river that crosses the plain about half a league away. All the ground here is trampled and broken, littered with shattered wagon wheels, splintered spears, and fractured shields made of wood and leather. There are no bodies, though. Soon enough, they come to the charred stump of a wild fig tree, and beside it the ruins of a stone shrine to some kind of river god. This is where they will camp, against all odds, outdoors but sheltered from the wind by the broken shrine. They are both asleep before the first stars appear.

THE NORTH WIND BLOWS and it's cold in the night, but Hani keeps snug in his brocaded robe, whose colors seem to seep into his dreams and wreathe a glowing Arinna in a shimmering rainbow. He wakes at dawn — the sun has yet to rise over the ruined city, but it has flung its own robe of gold across the bay and draped it over the crescent of hills lining the shore. From this vantage point he can see the sea beyond the bay. There is some sort of large structure, or maybe a row of buildings, down by the far western shore, beyond the river that crosses the sloping plain that separates the city from the sea. To the north, the water narrows into a long arm that winds away between the humped shores, but to the south it opens out wider and ever wider. A few islands huddle in its breast like sleeping turtles. It's true what they say — the sea goes on forever, farther than the eye can see. That is where the invaders came from when Hani was a baby, and that is where they have returned to, like wolves that converge upon a wounded fawn and then vanish into the woods when the carcass has been stripped clean. If he squints he can almost see their bone-white sails dropping below the horizon. Are they going home or to ruin a different city somewhere else? If he were them he'd be eager to return to hearth and farm and family after all these years, but maybe they aren't that kind of men. He wraps his arms around his knees and watches the day take shape, then rises to tend to the donkey.

As usual, she shows little sign of emotion beyond nuzzling him briefly under the chin, but her limp has taken a turn for the worse overnight and she is favoring her right foreleg, holding it so that only the toe of the hoof touches the ground. Whispering very gently in her ear, he asks her permission to inspect the injury, taking care to lift her leg above the fetlock and not to touch the hoof, because as loving as she may be, a donkey in pain will lash out at anyone without thinking twice about it. There's a large white stone embedded in the sole of her hoof, which is raw, inflamed, and bloody. It's a nasty wound that should have been attended to when it was fresh and clean. Hani suspects it's very painful, and he knows it's dangerous.

He will get only one chance at this, so he's got to get it right. He uses his one length of rope to secure her by the neck to the stump, loops his shawl around her right hind leg, and anchors it under a heavy cube of masonry that has tumbled from the shrine. She approaches and eyes him suspiciously, but she trusts him and submits. He cradles her injured leg in his hand as he whispers to her, takes a deep breath to steady his grip, then yanks the stone from her hoof without hesitation. She shivers and snorts but does not protest. Blood and pus spurt from the wound. If he were at home, Hani would treat it with a poultice of wolfsbane and marigold, but there's nothing like that here on this desolate plain, so he dresses the hoof in the shawl, which is all he can do. When he's done, his eye lights on the offending stone in the gravel and he picks it up. He finds that it's not a stone at all but a razor-sharp shard of human jawbone, with three molars still attached. He flings it into the rubble behind the shrine.

It takes him an hour or so to make his way back to the citadel. He tries to scout a source of clean water closer to their camping place, but all the wells in the upper city have been defiled. He fills both waterskins from the underground spring in the palace and drapes one over each shoulder. On his way back, he scavenges some radishes and spinach, a jar of olives, and a disc of soft cheese, wrapped in a fig leaf, from the overturned market stalls. Hoping to find a pair of sandals or work boots, he returns to the stable where he had seen great mounds of discarded children's clothing, but when he gets there he is overcome by a strange and sudden feeling of dread or alarm, and he leaves without making any selection.

This is the fourth time he has passed through this neighborhood, and he's beginning to recognize some of the corpses, especially those that are face up or contorted in some unique way. He does not expect them to have moved, of course, but their patience is still remarkable. What else is there for them to do but wait and rot? The weather has been cool, but every day brings summer a little closer, and this place, unwelcoming as it is now, will be totally foul before long, except to the rats and vultures.

Until her hoof has healed, he will have to do this heavy work without Ansa. It's strange being in the dead city without her. He hadn't realized how much he relies on her quiet strength, how so much of what he has seen he has seen through her eyes. When she's at his side, the whole world seems to pulse with hidden meaning and signs. It feels flatter without her, less telling. It makes him feel as if he has just now forgotten something he long thought he knew. He's been hearing about the war his whole life, and he thought he understood what it was, but now he sees he understands nothing. He looks around and asks himself: What happened here? He would be less confused if the donkey were at his side, not because she would have explained it to him, but because it would have been enough if at least one of them understood what was going on.

He rests at the top of the destroyed gatehouse. There is a word in the secret language — *kadingirra* — that means everything that can't be said in the secret language. You can only say beautiful things in the secret language, about love, kindness, friendship, courage, that sort of thing, so *kadingirra* means anything that you can only say in regular language because the secret language has no word for it. War, fear, anger, violence, disease — all those things are *kadingirra*. Because you can't talk about them, they don't exist in the world that the secret language describes — a world in which only Arinna, Hani, and the god who invented the secret language live. That world and everything in it is called *assiyatar* — the opposite of *kadingirra*. *Assiyatar* exists only when you are speaking the secret language, which both creates it and describes it. *Kadingirra* rules everywhere else.

Hani surveys the carnage below. What did the people who did this think they were doing? If someone had stopped them for one moment and said, "What's the point of all this? What are you trying to accomplish?" and they had actually paused in their rampage and thought about it and tried to give an honest answer, what would they have said? What could they have said, with their own wives and mothers and sisters and daughters waiting for them at home? Is it possible they enjoyed doing it? Hani has killed many animals in his life but he has not yet ever felt the urge to kill a person. Even when he was bullied and battered by his brothers, and Father stood by and let it happen, his anger and humiliation had not turned in that direction. He did not become like them, and that only made them uglier. He wonders if it's just a matter of time, if it's one of those things that comes naturally once you reach a certain age, like growing hair on your body, but looking around him he thinks he understands that war is not about the killing. It seems to him that it must be about fear more than anything. The people who did this went about it so thoroughly that they must have been deeply afraid of something. But what could make them this scared? Children are afraid of monsters, women are afraid of men, but men seem mostly to be afraid of themselves, which is probably why they spend so much of their lives in terror of one sort or another. That sounds about right. Hani remembers one of his uncles once telling him very seriously that the world is a galloping horse with no reins. "You have to mount it, ride it hard, and hold on for dear life." But this is probably not what he meant.

In only the few hours that Hani has been gone, Ansa's condition has deteriorated. Her legs are stiff, her nostrils are flared, the muscles of her jaw and shoulders are shaken by rippling spasms. He tries to put his ear to her chest, but she shies away from even his gentlest touch. He has seen this before, and it's not good. He hopes it's not lockjaw, but it could well be. You never can tell with a donkey; they're hard to read and often show no signs of distress until it's too late to help. He rummages in his bag for a stub of bread, crushes it into a handful of crumbs, and scatters them on the embers of last night's campfire with a muttered prayer to Telipinu. If Telipinu really exists and he is listening, Hani knows that the god will detect his lack of sincerity, but if it's not better than nothing, it can't be worse.

He sets Ansa up with a pail of water and all the vegetables he has scavenged from the city. The day is not going to be a hot one, but even so he fashions a canopy for her by tenting the robe from the top of the shrine to the tree stump. Her third eyelid is showing and he thinks she may be growing sensitive to the light and the drying wind. If she's seriously ill, the next twelve hours will tell, and he wants her to be as comfortable as she can possibly be in the meantime.

Hani knows that he needs to return to the dead city right away, that if he's to have any chance of finding Arinna he has got to take advantage of the cool weather before the corpses begin to rot in earnest and attract scavengers. He knows, too, that there's little he can do for Ansa now and that his hovering presence is only likely to upset her in her current condition. But he can hardly bear the thought of going back to the city to begin the house-by-house search that he will need to do if he hopes to track Arinna down. It's not just the prospect of days spent navigating the narrow alleys, with their stink of charred timber and their shadows heavy with threat, that has sapped him of his will. Yes, he's scared, he's been scared every moment since they took to the road. He's scared even though he's growing more convinced by the minute that there's no one left alive except Arinna and him. And he's even more scared that Arinna may not be alive at all and that he could stumble across her tiny, grinning corpse around any corner. But it's not fear that's holding him back. He's ashamed to admit it even to himself, but the fact is he's more upset about the likelihood that Ansa is dangerously sick than he is about anything else that has happened since he left the valley. Could it really be that he values the life of one aging donkey over those of hundreds of dead people, most of them harmless old folk, even if they are strangers? Who ever heard of anything so nasty and pathetic? There's no one anywhere to watch and judge him here, but still he feels like someone is standing right behind him and looking deep into his heart and seeing all the ugliness there. Hani knows that he must be a bad person, the very bad person his father has often told him he is, but it doesn't make him want to cling to Ansa any less tightly. It doesn't change the fact that his heart aches with love for her and that he would gladly sacrifice all the strangers in the world if that would help her recover. This is always the problem when you love so few people in the world, and two are dead and one is a donkey. You get scared. It just makes him feel weak and wobbly, because everyone knows that only the good are courageous, and that is why he can't face returning to the city today, because he's not good and he's not even that sorry about it.

He remembers the mysterious structures he glimpsed by the shore of the bay that morning. Whatever it is down there, it would have made sense for anyone trying to escape the city to flee in that direction, so that's where he'll go. Secretly, he hopes that Arinna isn't there, because it's exhausting to always be worrying about finding something that you're not sure you want to find—except it's not "secretly" since he just admitted it to himself. He sets off with a loaf of bread, a little cheese, and a bladder of water. There are three pairs of frog legs left that he will save for his supper.

The trail descends to a ford in the river, then veers north toward the bay. It's a well-worn track, probably used by cattle herders for generations. What surprises him is the clear evidence etched into the ground that, where now there is nothing but a trampled, barren expanse of lifeless rubble, there were once paths and houses branching off either side of the road. No walls or fences are left standing, only the chalky profiles of long-gone foundations, wells, enclosures, the pale ghosts of tracks and courtyards outlined in dust and weeds. The settlements that once stood out here in the open must have been the first to be swept away when the war broke out all those years ago. On a farm, you grow up knowing that the idea of safety is an illusion, a story you tell yourself so you can sleep at night. It's strange to think that this place was once so prosperous and secure that people believed they were able to live safely beyond the protection of the ramparts. What did they think when the invaders appeared suddenly on the horizon one day and crowded their ships into the mouth of the bay and hauled them row on row onto the beach and set up camp and perimeters, and their watch fires burned all that night like a deadly noose along the shoreline? Hani can imagine those long-dead homesteaders standing silently right here, in their pig sties and kitchen gardens, their hands shielding their squinting eyes against the glitter of the sun on the surf as Hani is doing himself right now, and wondering, wondering. Even when things are simple it's often so hard to understand what's going on. This would not have been something their sheltered lives had prepared them for. Did they mistake the strangers for friends, or did they know even then that the beginning of the end of the world was at hand? Did they turn around to see their own sentinels lining the city walls, craning their necks and nervously palming their lances, and did they sense the watchmen's perplexity and terror and lose heart?

When you play a game of knucklebones, or you wrestle inside a ring, or you run a foot race against your friends, you know exactly when it's over and who has won. War seems like it's more complicated. It feels fuzzy around the edges, like it's hard to tell exactly when it started and you never can be sure if it has ended. Is the war over now? When he finds Arinna and they return to the valley, will everything be different than it has been? Will things somehow go back to the way they were before he was born, whatever that was? Life lived by the rhythm of the seasons, maybe, men and women and children living out their natural spans, not cut down by violence or starvation or despair? The old ways restored, rituals, rites, and celebrations performed with joy and hope? Or will home never be more than a shadow of what it used to be, a sorry excuse for a healthy, happy country, like old Labarna, who was badly mauled in a tussle with a wild boar in his childhood and has carried the jagged scars on his body and in his soul ever since? Hani has heard people talk about peace his whole life, but he doesn't really know what it means or what it would be like. Everyone assumes it's better than war, but how would you know? Talk of peace is like talk of a king's banquet, made up in equal parts of hearsay, imagination, and hunger, but maybe peace isn't a thing at all, maybe it's no different a way of life than any other, except for how you picture it in your head. Here, right now, you could say the city is peaceful, from a certain point of view. There's quiet and rest, no fighting, no sorrow; it's not all that different from what you find in nature, some things dying and other things growing in their place. Animals fight and starve and kill each other, but nobody calls that war. They call it nature; they call it beautiful. Maybe peace is not a way of living but a way of thinking? Or maybe not. Maybe he will not be allowed to find Arinna until he's sure the war is over, and he's not convinced he will ever know for certain when that happens, no matter how long this drags on. As far as he can tell, there isn't a whole lot of difference between war and peace.

It's all downhill from the city to the shore, a gentle slope extending across several leagues, with not a tree, shrub, or stone bigger than Hani's head to interrupt it. Almost nothing is growing here, even though it's high spring and the soil appears to be fertile. It looks like a giant has farted on the land and poisoned every living thing. Hani has spent time among the horse breeders of his country and watched them at their work, running horses through their paces at the end of a long rope within fenced paddocks until every last blade of grass and dandelion has been trampled into the dust. This plain looks like that only a thousand times worse, as far as the eye can see. The north wind is still blowing, but there's nothing — not a leaf, not a branch, not even a stump — to catch at it and make it whistle or thrum. The silence is eerie and unnerving, as still and deathlike as anything he has ever seen. He tries to hum a tune but his breath dries and crackles on his lips. There is no one alive for miles and miles in any direction, yet he feels threatened and finds his fist squeezed around the cords of his sling. But he has never been so alone in his life, or so safe from ambush.

Hani wonders if he could really be the last person left alive. This isn't the first time he's asked himself that question, but it's the first time he's felt like he needs to give it some real consideration. He rotates slowly on the axis of his body — west, south, east, north, west. Nothing moves, not a single hearth fire sends a column of smoke into the empty sky, the sea is a desert, its shores trace the outline of a murdered continent. When he left the valley there were still a few people scratching out a livelihood from the soil, but they were mostly old women and children, and he has seen what has become of such people in every community he has happened upon. It would be perfectly reasonable to assume that everyone in the valley is dead by now. In his heart he won't yet believe it, and can't for Arinna's sake, but he has lived his whole life studying and interpreting the evidence that nature has placed before him, so it's only a matter of time and more of the same until he'll be forced to admit himself convinced that he is well and truly alone here, if not everywhere. When even the grown men of this city have been ground into the dust of war, what chance does a six-year-old girl have?

What would it be like to be the only person left alive, on this side of the sea or the other? Hani has never had a problem keeping himself busy. Unlike most of his friends, he doesn't get lonely and he's happy to spend his days by himself, with only his thoughts for company. The truth is, except for knucklebones, most children's games and most children themselves bore him and he wouldn't miss them if he never saw them again, with a few exceptions. The problem is, there are no exceptions when the world comes to an end. You don't get to choose. The only way you get to be the most powerful human being on earth is when you're the only human being on earth, and you are alone forever, not just while you're on a fishing expedition or whatever, with your little sister waiting for you at home with the snail shell she has found and saved especially for you. For all he knows, she's there right now while he's here looking for her, but it can't be helped. He has to be here, end of the world or not.

A bee buzzes by right under his nose and goes on its way to who knows where. How strange to see a bee here of all places. This plain should be covered in wildflowers at this time of year, but it's barren and brown. How far will the bee have to travel to find even a tiny nip of pollen? Surely it will tumble from the air in exhaustion before it finds anything to eat. Or maybe it's not looking for a flower. Hani recalls how the mother goddess Hannahanna sent a bee to search for the missing god Telipinu, patron of farmers. When Telipinu disappeared, the windows became clogged with mist and smoke filled the houses. Logs were smothered on the hearth; the gods were suffocated on the altars. The ewe rejected her lamb and the cow rejected her calf. Humans and gods starved to death. The bee eventually found Telipinu and stung him and smeared him all over with wax, and Telipinu was so enraged that he began to wreak havoc on the world. Hani scans the landscape of devastation around him, sees in his mind's eye the death and destruction behind him. The bee, he realizes, is not on a mission to find Telipinu; it has already found him and stung him.

The trail leads Hani to the edge of the river and a ford where the water runs clear and clean beneath a thicket of stunted tamarisks that have somehow endured. He goes down on his hands and knees and drinks like an animal, dunking his head in the icy stream and washing his neck. He refills the waterskin. By the side of the road overlooking the ford is a barrow, the only spot in all the surrounding area that is still covered with grass. Back home in the valley, the lord Tarhuntassa is buried under just such a mound, so Hani guesses that this, too, is the tomb of an ancient king. There's nothing to identify him, no column or marker of any kind, so now that all his people have been slaughtered or scattered, no one will ever know who he was or what he did, no matter how great he may have been in his own time. He's now just one of the nameless dead, like everyone else, and his deeds have been carried off on the north wind like chaff. Worse yet, now that there's no one left to remember him, he's alone forever. Back at home, your cremated remains are sealed in a jar with a double layer of fat to keep them dry, and stored in a communal cave with the ashes of all your clan and ancestors. Not everyone agrees that it's a good thing to spend eternity in the company of your extended family, but it has to be better than spending it alone and forsaken in the middle of a windswept plain. You will never be forgotten anyhow, if that matters to you, for the dead are jealous of their own and have far longer memories than the living.

Beyond the barrow and across the river, the distant structures that Hani glimpsed from the brow of the slope come into clearer view. He sees now that they are not buildings but long sections of a wooden palisade that runs parallel to the beach for half a league or more. Someone has torn parts of it down or burned it at random intervals. Between the palisade and the shore are tall, oddly shaped skeletal constructions that, as he approaches, turn out to be the carcasses of abandoned ships lying atilt in rows, their masts pointing into the sky in all directions like accusing fingers, some bearing the tattered remnants of pennants fluttering in the breeze. Even closer, he sees that there is a deep trench protecting the palisade along its entire length, and that the banks of the trench are lined with sharpened stakes. Closer still, it is revealed that the trench is lined with human bones, many still connected to one another in crazy, jigging skeletons with their hilarious skulls attached. Unlike the bodies in the city, these have clearly been lying here for some time, years maybe, telling the story of a battle that took place at some earlier phase of the war. He's now near enough to the beach to hear the tide hissing and clattering through the shale, and when he narrows his eyes to slits he can make it look as if the skeletons are breathing and sighing at one another, sorrowful and resigned to their fate.

He turns to follow the course of the trench, seeking a way across and into the graveyard of ships, which would be a good place for a nimble, quick-witted survivor to hide and shelter. He tries not to let his eyes wander to the bottom of the trench, but they have a mind of their own. Except for one stylish skeleton in a cap of polecat fur, the dead are very naked, clothed only in the shame of the defeated. Hani remembers being told by some old man who had fought in a long-forgotten conflict that the only thing that distinguishes one soldier from another is his armor. "Strip them of their armor and you can't tell friend from foe. They're all lying out there side by side in the dust and no one knows who's who." Hani thinks of that now that he sees them all stripped not only of their armor but of their flesh. He wonders if any of them ever thought about what they would look like when they became naked skeletons on the battlefield. He tries to imagine himself as a skeleton; he knows his bones are inside him somewhere because he can feel them under his skin, but even so how funny it must be to be a skeleton! Every single skeleton looks exactly like every other skeleton. You can't even tell the difference between a man and woman—although he doubts there are any woman skeletons lying around in this trench—and you have no idea what the person was like who once moved around in it. When he tries to imagine each of them, with their own names and mothers and fathers and childhoods and favorite foods and secret fears and jokes they played on their friends, it makes him lightheaded. It's not a good or helpful way to think about the unclaimed dead.

Finally, he comes to a gap in the trench that leads to a smashed gate in the palisade, hanging off its leather hinges. On the other side lie the dead ships, most of them stripped of their planks or burned down to their beams and left to molder where they were first hauled up on the sand all those years ago. There are dozens of them, each bigger than the biggest barn Hani has ever seen, but you can see the deep gouges in the sand where others were dragged back into the sea to make the return journey home. The invaders would have known from the very beginning that they'd need fewer ships to get home in than they did to get here. There are no bodies anywhere in sight. They must have cremated all their dead outside the camp where they ate and slept, as anyone would. And there is no Arinna. This is the first time he has spoken above a whisper in many days. His voice sounds squeaky and unnatural, like that of a wounded animal, when he calls out for her, again and again.

When he reaches the end of the row of ships, he slips out of his loincloth, turns his feet to the surf, and wades out, and when he's in up to his waist he plunges. He's surprised to find that the sea is warmer than the river back home, which descends from the snowcapped mountains. It also tastes salty, which he has been told about but didn't believe until now. When he opens his eyes under water, it's not as clear or bright as the river, but he can see fish and green plants anchored to the sandy bottom, which throws off rolling plumes of grit as the waves rock back and forth, back and forth. Hani lifts his feet and wraps his arms around his knees, bobbing like an apple just below the surface and listening to the dreamlike growl and sigh of the surf. Swimming in the sea is very different from swimming in the river, which always has somewhere it wants to take you to. The river knows exactly where it comes from and where it's going, but the sea is everywhere and nowhere at the same time, and for that reason it doesn't seem to have anywhere else it needs to be. Hani likes it. And the sea talks to you where the river guards its secrets.

When he has swum to his heart's content, he walks back along the waterline to where the palisade meets the shore, then swims around its underwater rump and reemerges on the open plain. He shades his eyes with the palm of his hand and scans the upland for a sight of the city ramparts. At this distance it's hard to make out, the gray limestone of the walls blending naturally into the burnt henna of the grassless plain. It looks like a sleeping lion, its body wrapped around its most recent kill, guarding it jealously. Eager to avoid the gruesome trench, he decides to follow the shoreline to the mouth of the river, cross there, then trek the eastern bank of the river upstream to the ford.

The river here is not a single channel but a broad estuary of outstretched fingers reaching into the sea. It's too shallow to swim and the bed is muddy with silt that sucks at his feet, slowing his progress. He's not halfway across when the water begins to rise rapidly from the direction of the bay, surging and churning at his knees and thighs, and then, within minutes, swirling at his hips and seeming to charge at his legs while trying to pull them out from under him at the same time, like a wrestler swiping at his heels while pressing against his waist. Hani slogs forward, twisting at the hips as he struggles to pull each foot from the mud, clawing at the current. There is a sandbank only thirty strides ahead, but the water is rising faster than he is advancing toward it, and it is bellowing like a bull. His outstretched fingertip touches something slimy, and then his entire lower body is enveloped in a writhing mass of gleaming eels, so thick that the river bottom is completely obscured, and then they're gone. Hani's breath comes in ragged gasps. If he stumbles, or the water reaches his mouth before he gets to safety, he will not be able to right himself. And even as this thought comes to him he's knocked over by a powerful breaker and loses his footing, and that is what saves him, because it reminds him that wrestling with gods is a fool's game and that he's perfectly capable of floating himself away from this confrontation. And so he does, the tide roaring in his ears as he splays his limbs and the river, now his ally, buoys him swiftly to a backwater lined with deervetch and galingale. He lies there, his back resting against the warm sand, while he recovers his breath.

When he gets to his feet, he finds that his loincloth has been swept away by the current. He's not sure if his survival represents a defeat or a victory, but either way he finds to his pleasure, as he dries off in the pulsing breeze, that his nakedness, unseen and possibly never to be seen by anyone ever again, is not a burden. Not since he was a toddler has he walked naked across open ground, but he finds it eerily normal, as if it's all happening in a dream.

The sun is preparing to set into the open sea when he reaches the shrine. Ansa is lying on her side under the tenting, her legs rigid, her pretty muzzle coated in dust. The wound on her hoof is beginning to smell and may already be infested with maggots. She has touched neither food nor water, and her third eyelid is protruding and bright pink. Foam bubbles on her lips and seizures ripple through her muscles from neck to croup. She's unable to lift her head, but she follows him with her left eye as he places the pail by her muzzle, then sits himself cross-legged behind her and lifts her head gently onto his lap. He reaches up and tears a ragged scrap from the robe, which he dips into the pail and dabs at her mouth. She will not drink, he knows, but he hopes that it will bring her some comfort in her final moments to be reminded that she is beloved and not alone. Because she is so much wiser than him, he believes she knows this already, but there can be nothing else for him to do for the next few hours. As he cradles her head in his lap and scratches the scalp between her ears, his mind wanders over the years they have known each other and all that she has taught him. He's sure she remembers the time long ago, after Arinna had taken a tumble from her back, that she pledged to always keep Arinna safe from that day forward, and how Arinna then made him promise that he would never let anything bad happen to Ansa. Hani is pretty sure that Ansa is too profound to allow little things like broken promises to disturb her, but he does not remind her of that day, just in case.

When the first stars appear, rising freshly washed and sparkling from the sea, he's still humming the lullabies he remembers his mother singing to Arinna, and when he senses the half moon rising at his back and he sees its light fall on the distant shoreline, catching the crest of each motionless wave as the scales of a trout hook the sunlight when it leaps from the water, he tells Ansa the few stories he knows about Arma the moon god. The stories ring a little stale and pointless in his ears, but it's the sound of his voice in this new wilderness that matters now to them both.

THERE'S NOT ENOUGH WOOD to build a funeral pyre, and even if there were, Hani is not strong enough to move Ansa's body. He could spend days trying to dig a grave to protect her from scavengers, but the ground here is rock hard and he has no metal tools. Instead, he will build a cairn to serve her as both burial mound and monument.

As he gathers suitable stones, he tries to imagine what Father and the other men of the valley would say if they knew that he was building a shrine to a donkey. If they saw him at this work, first they would goggle, then they'd laugh, then they'd be furious, and then they'd beat him, just as they beat Ansa for minor errors, or momentary mulishness, or just for nothing at all, her whole life. His father especially would feel nothing but shame and anger over his son's love for a dumb animal. A domestic beast is for labor and pro-creation and meat, and nothing more, he'd tell him. An animal has no soul. It's an insult to the gods to treat it the same way you treat a human being. That's why Hani and Arinna never shared how they felt and what they knew about Ansa with the others — that she did have a soul, and a great one, greater than those of just about anyone in the valley and maybe beyond. Hani didn't even know how to describe her to himself, and he had had to go out and find the fancy words that best fit her, because her qualities were so unfamiliar to the locals that they had no name for them. But he knew, he was convinced, that she was endowed with the kind of wisdom, and forbearance, and fortitude, and compassion that made her superior to all those who harmed and cursed her — that made her almost divine in her own right. Everything she had, all those long words for something simple and true, Hani wants. Everything she was, Hani hopes one day to be. If anyone Hani knows deserves a memorial, it is Ansa, and he intends to give her one, no matter what anyone might have to say about it. And since there's no one around to object, and there may never again be anyone around to object — just as there's no one left to be offended by his nakedness — he gets to it. New world, new rules.

The task takes most of the day; by the time he's finished, his hands have been rubbed raw and the oblong cairn has risen to chest height. His heart feels as if it were filled with black waves crashing against its inner walls, pushed before an icy wind. He squats in the shadow of the shrine and weeps silently as he finishes off the last of the frog legs. They've turned gamy but he doesn't care, even when he vomits them up a few minutes later. He still has plenty of bread, the uneaten vegetables, and a bag of barley groats, if he can find something to cook them in. And he isn't hungry anyway. He knocks back half a waterskin and recalls the pleasure of the frog hunt as if it were a hundred years ago. That was in a world where the city still loomed fantastic and mysterious in his imagination, where he still believed that anything might happen on this adventure, and where Ansa was still alive.

He's tempted to take Ansa's death as a sign that it's time to call the whole thing off. He's been stupid, as usual, stupid and selfish. Ansa is dead, Huzzi and Arnu are dead, Father is dead. Arinna must be dead, too. What's the point? Who is being loyal to whom? The war is over, the city is ruined and abandoned, and it's not too late to get some of the summer wheat in the ground if he gives up now and goes home where he's needed. That is what anyone with half a brain would do. As if in response to his thoughts, a gust of wind picks up a swirling cone of dust and dances it across the slope. He watches the whirlwind as it skips away toward the southern edge of the city and dissipates, and it occurs to him that this may be Ansa speaking to him through the wind. It's only an idle thought, and a foolish one at that, but it reminds him that she would not have allowed him to give up after one setback, no matter how crushing, under any circumstances. She would have said something like, "Anything worth finding is worth looking for," or "It's precisely because you're not likely to find Arinna alive that you need to keep looking for her," or "You can't be true to Arinna until you are true to yourself," or something clever he could never have come up with himself and would barely have understood. Whatever it was, she would have been right, and he would have heeded her advice. He can't go home until the war is over, and as far as he's concerned the war won't be over until he has found Arinna, because finding Arinna is his war. It makes no difference if she's dead or alive.

He gathers up his remaining supplies. His knapsack is heavier now that he's carrying Ansa's load as well as his own, but it's nothing he can't handle, and it gets a little lighter every day. What he needs to do now is find a new place to make camp, somewhere outside the city walls but not too far outside, and convenient to a water source that doesn't require daily expeditions through the slaughter zone. He follows the path mapped out by the whirlwind, and in ten minutes he finds himself standing at the great southern gate to the city. It's bigger than any of the others and must have been the main entry point for anyone coming from the harbor or places south. Hani knows nothing about warfare or its tactics, but just one look at the gatehouse makes it very clear that this would have been the chief target of all the invaders' attempts to break into the city. It's the closest gate to the water and offers a straight line from the enemy's encampment on the beach to the city walls. It would have been the first thing they saw when they disembarked from wherever it was they came from. Twenty cubits in front of the gate stands a long, curved stone barrier, some ten hands high, that was clearly designed to break a cavalry charge and prevent a direct assault on the gate. There's nothing about the gate that suggests weakness or vulnerability, which makes it all the stranger to see it fully intact, the massive gatehouse and watchtower undamaged and its great wooden doors still on their hinges and agape. It's almost as if someone had opened them wide to the invading army. In the guardroom, there's a full rack of pristine spears, no sign of violence or panicked rout, and even a cot in the corner. The room still smells of the sweaty, unwashed men who occupied it just a few days ago. Hani helps himself to a swig of fresh wine from a jug left on a windowsill, but it's undiluted and he spits it out. He doesn't need to think twice about it — the guardroom will make a perfect place to camp, and it even offers shelter from the elements. And if he can't find a well within the city that hasn't been polluted, it's barely half a league from here to the river. He drops his belongings on the cot and heads through the interior courtyard and into the city.

The first thing he notices is that there are no bodies anywhere in sight. No bodies, no looted market stalls, no incinerated buildings, no putrid vapors wafting on the breeze. Just silence and emptiness. This must have been a very strange war. Hani listens for the story the silence is trying to tell him, but he can't make it out at all. There's something dreadful about it, something sinister, somehow even worse than the clotted carnage of the upper city, which at least tells its own story openly and honestly. There is death here just the same, and terror, but they have cloaked themselves, like a mountain lion crouched and quivering with murderous intent just a few paces from an unsuspecting fawn. Hani doesn't like it, not one bit. He does not sense that he himself is in any danger, that he's being stalked; instead, he somehow hears the slashing of blades, the shrieks of the fallen, the wailing of mothers and the muffled grunts of foot soldiers sating their bloodlust ring out through this unnatural silence.

A broad, cobbled street leads in a gentle, undulating slope from the gate toward the upper city; narrow dirt alleys lined with brick-and-clay huts branch off on either side. There will be hundreds of such dwellings within the confines of the city walls. If Arinna does not answer his calls, he will have to investigate each and every one. But for now he has lost his voice and that will have to wait.

It's not until he reaches a crossroads five minutes north of the gatehouse that he stumbles upon his first corpse. He sees its legs sticking out from behind the stone parapet of a well at the center of the crossroads. Its feet are clad in sturdy buskins of a kind that Hani has not seen before. They will make a valuable addition to his gear. He circles the well until he finds himself face-to-face with the corpse, which is propped up against the parapet, its legs splayed, a livid wound running up the inside of its left thigh and under its tunic, which is dark with brown blood from the waist down. The corpse wears a dagger in an embossed and bejeweled leather scabbard hanging from a baldric slung across its shoulder. Its eyes are closed and its head droops like a garden poppy heavy with seed. This is one of the few dead soldiers Hani has encountered since his arrival in the city, and the only one he has examined up close. It looks as if it were asleep.

Hani kneels at its feet and begins to unlace the buskins. They are beautifully made, by far the nicest shoes he will ever wear no matter how long he lives, with several layers of soft calfskin for the soles and decorative scrolls on the uppers, but the laces are complex and tightly knotted halfway up the shins. He finds himself trying to work them cautiously, as if he's afraid of waking the owner. As he picks at a knot with his fingernails, he wonders about the dead soldier. Was he one of theirs or one of ours? His hair is dark brown, long and braided like that of many men from the valley, but Hani has no idea what the invaders look like, since all he's seen of them so far is skeletons. Maybe their hair is exactly the same. The soldier's tunic could be from anywhere. He does not have a shield, which might have revealed something about where he was from, but since Hani doesn't know anything about shields it probably wouldn't have helped anyway. Whoever he was, he was young and quite handsome, with features more delicate than are commonly seen in the valley, and he died in a lot of pain and, like as not, a long way from home. Rich, too, judging by his trimmings. Hani tries to focus on the shoes. The leather laces are warm from the late-afternoon sun but they are stubborn, and he clicks his tongue and tosses his head in exasperation. That is when he sees that the corpse has opened its eyes and is watching him impassively.

He flies straight through the city gate and out onto the open plain, stopping only when he reaches the stone barrier. He flings himself behind it, peeks over the top to make sure he hasn't been followed, and collapses to the ground, gasping and trembling. As the fear catches up with him, it wipes his mind of thought. From here he can see across the sweep of the plain and the bay to the group of islands clustered along the horizon, but they do nothing to reassure him. His heartbeat remains fierce and insistent even as the rhythm of his breathing returns to normal and the sweat dries on his body.

What has just happened? It feels as if everything that has taken place over the past days — his decision to leave the valley, the frog hunt, the journey along the river, the weir, his first view of the city, the butchery, the graveyard of the ships, the battle with the river, the death of Ansa — is wrapped up in the split second when his gaze met that of the dead soldier. Nothing else has happened to him in his whole life except that moment and everything else. But what exactly has happened? How does he find himself cowering behind this wall, his heart rattling the bars of its cage like a trapped bear?

There was a crossroads in the empty city. There was the silence of death.

But what happened?

There was a soldier. A dead soldier, wearing boots.

There were boots, good boots. One was laced to a leg that was gashed open from knee to groin.

There were knotted laces and dried blood.

The dead man woke up. The dead man woke up and looked him in the eye.

It occurs to Hani that he's no longer the sole survivor of the end of the world. Only a moment before the corpse opened its eyes, he had pictured himself striding through the new world in all his naked glory in his magnificent new buskins. Now there will be neither new buskins nor new world, only the prospect of having to share the old world with a living corpse.

He tries to remember if he screamed when the dead man woke up. He doesn't think so, but he did fall backward and cushioned his landing with the palms of his hands, which are bleeding and still embedded with gravel. Did the dead soldier move in any way? He didn't even blink. Had his eyes been open all along? Had he died with them open, but Hani just hadn't noticed? Maybe, but no—the soldier had looked as if he were sleeping, and even sleeping peacefully at that, Hani remembers thinking. Could his head have been tilted at a slightly different angle, could he have raised it just a little bit before opening his eyes, even if Hani didn't see him do it? Now that Hani thinks about it, the dead man's lips were badly chapped and swollen, which they wouldn't have been if he had died two or three days ago. And the color of his wound — the wound of a man who had died several days earlier wouldn't be bright red and purple, would it?

What happened, it's beginning to look like, is not that Hani awakened a dead man. It's that Hani awakened a man who wasn't dead yet. So it's true. There is a survivor, and it's a soldier. That doesn't necessarily mean that the war isn't over. One soldier can't fight a war by himself, because there's no one for him to fight against. But what if the soldier is the Akhillisa? He doesn't look anything like the monster that haunted the nightmares of Hani's childhood, but maybe this is a disguise he uses to lure his victims to their deaths. Maybe he's one of those half-man, half-bear creatures that stalk the mountain forests — man in the sunlight and bear in the moonlight. If Arinna were here she'd know instantly if he was the Akhillisa or not, but Hani doesn't have her special instinct for seeing the world without its veils.

The problem is, the dead soldier is definitely not the only survivor, because Hani is a survivor, too. From everything he's seen, soldiers — especially the soldiers who ruined this city — are happy to chop down the unarmed and the elderly if there are no enemy soldiers around to chop down. And who knows what they do with the young women and children, since there don't seem to be any among the dead? So if the dead soldier that Hani woke up today — the not-dead soldier — is one of them, and especially if he's the Akhillisa, wounded but still hungering for human flesh, he will want to kill Hani as soon as he's capable of doing it. He has the dagger to do it with, too. True, Hani has his sling, and he's pretty good with it, but as his brothers always used to say, you don't bring a sling to a knife fight. Hani wouldn't bring his little flint blade to a knife fight, either, and he definitely wouldn't bring a sling to any kind of fight with the Akhillisa, because the Akhillisa would ram it up his ass and use it as a spit to slow-roast him over an open fire. Anyway, the knife and the sling are both in Hani's knapsack, which is in the guardroom, which is in the city where the Akhillisa is even now whetting his dagger on a cobblestone and dreaming of bloodbaths. Sure, he may look like he's at death's door, but as a sworn enemy to frogs and crows Hani knows all too well how cunning and deceitful enemies can be when they want to be. He has seen plovers pretend to be hurt to distract predators from their nestlings. Maybe the Akhillisa isn't wounded at all but is just trying to lull Hani into a false sense of security. But even if he's not pretending, and he's just a mortal man, that would still mean that the war isn't over, only now the only combatants left are a dying soldier and a boy with a sling. Is this what people mean when they talk about peace? Maybe peace is just war taking a rest. Maybe war never really ends. A caterpillar and a butterfly are the same animal that goes by two different names. Peace and war.

On the other hand, it could be that the dying soldier is on Hani's side, whatever that means, but how can you tell? He looks just like someone Hani might know, if a little more like a nobleman than a farmer, but maybe the invaders look like Hani, too. Hani has heard all sorts of crazy stories about them—how they are so ugly they make their own mothers cry when they're born; how they feast on the raw entrails of pigs, and as a result always have tapeworms dangling from their butts like tails; how the sound of their language can kill a goose at thirty paces—but who knows what to believe anymore? For sure, the best way to tell would be to get him to say something, and if he speaks barbarian talk then... then what? What is Hani going to do? Sneak up on him with his sling at the ready, trick him into saying something, and crack him one between the eyes? Hani is pretty sure he could do some serious damage, and possibly even kill someone at close enough range, but that holds no interest for him, even if the soldier is the Akhillisa. His brothers would jump at the chance to do something like that to a wounded, defenseless stranger, even if they weren't sure he deserved it, but it only makes Hani feel sick and a little sad. He shakes his head just to clear it of the image.

The sun is preparing itself to sink into the sea, and he has some decisions to make. He's hungry, but his food is in the guardroom. He's thirsty, but his water bag is in the guardroom. The night promises to be cold again, but his scavenged robe is in the guardroom. He's in danger, but his sling is in the guardroom. The decision would seem to be an easy one, but he can't decide to make it. Of course he's afraid to return to the city, but the problem is not that he's afraid; even the bravest man in the world doesn't take unnecessary risks. The soldier certainly looked seriously wounded, and he's almost definitely unable to walk on that leg, but if Hani can't even tell the difference between a dead man and a live one he could easily have misjudged the gravity of the injury, too.

He will wait until it's dark to retrieve his belongings from the guardroom. He has excellent night vision, and the half moon will give him all the light he needs. Of course, it will also betray him if his enemy is on the prowl, but that can't be helped—he can't stay hungry, cold, naked, and unarmed forever. He's pretty confident he can outrun any assailant in a pinch, except maybe a bear-man.

He's awakened not by hunger, thirst, or cold in the middle of the clear night but by an idea that comes to him in a dream. The dream is muddy but the idea is clear as river water. He can end the war. The power to end the war and restore the world is in his hands. All he has to do is grab his things and go home. This much he has learned—so long as there are two people left anywhere on earth, they will find each other and fight each other and the war will go on. That's how it's always been with men and gods, as far as he can tell. But if Hani simply refuses to fight, the war will have to come to an end. If he leaves now, in the middle of the night, the soldier will never find him, and even if he does somehow manage to track him down, Hani will just keep moving on and hiding and moving on again until the soldier gives up and goes home. And in this way Hani will end the war that has been raging since he was a baby, and probably long before that, maybe since the beginning of time. It's such a simple idea he can't believe no one's ever thought of it before.

His heart roars, then whimpers. How could he have forgotten, even for a passing moment, why he's here and who he's here for? What kind of a brother forgets his own sister? Hani is furious and disgusted with himself. If the choice is between ending the war and rescuing Arinna, no matter how slim the chance, it's no choice at all. If Ansa were here, she'd remind him of that every time he allowed himself to be sidetracked, and in the end she would make him the steadfast and true brother that Arinna deserves. Alone, he's weak and easily distracted by shiny things, so he has to make doubly sure to keep a strict eye on himself. Having almost failed her this once, he'll need to be on his guard against allowing it to happen a second time. And in this fresh resolve, under the bright moonlight and washed in the cool breath of the sleeping plain, he scurries from the cover of the barrier, scuttles in a fluid crouch across the open ground to the gate, and sidles his way soundlessly into the guardroom. Two minutes later, he's back behind the barrier, wrapped in his robe and ripping at the hardened bread with his bare teeth.

He awakens to the rising sun, and now the plan is complete. If Hani can't end the war by running away, then the dying soldier must die. It's not a choice but the only option available. It's the only way to end the war and save Arinna at the same time, presuming she's still alive. Hani will kill the soldier, and he will do it without waiting around to figure out which side he belongs to. The mere thought of it makes him feel sick to his stomach, but he's pretty sure he can do it because it needs to be done. Today, now, before his courage deflates, he will make his way through the narrow alleys and approach the crossroads from an unexpected direction. Concealed in the shadows, he will take careful aim with his sling and smack the dying soldier right between the eyes with a smooth stone. While the soldier lies stunned, Hani will rush him and kill him with his own dagger or the flint, either across the throat or in the heart, whichever comes most naturally in the moment. And then he will despoil his defeated enemy of his shoes and his weapon, as is his right. It all sounds so simple and easy when he goes over it in his imagination, but Hani is not kidding himself. He has never killed a person before and he does not pretend that he's some big hero who can do it like plucking a chicken. He won't get any pleasure out of it, the way a lot of people he knows would do or claim to have done. He's killed plenty of animals, big and small, because that's what you have to do on a farm, like it or not, but he doesn't fool himself that killing a man at close range will be anything like that. Yet it has to be done for Arinna's sake. He just hopes he can get it over with before the soldier has a chance to say anything.

He washes down some bread with water and grabs his sling. He raises his head above the rim of the barrier, scans the gate and walls for any sign of life, then takes the gate at full tilt. Once in the city, he turns down the first alley to his left, which curves northward as it follows the arc of the city wall. He slows to a creep, careful to listen for any telltale sounds as he passes the open windows and doorways of the huts or scrambles through them and out the back. These hovels must have been home to the poorest of the poor. Apparently, in the city as on the farm, the common folk all live together at one end and the rich all live together at the other. Here in the lower city, most homes have only the most threadbare straw sacks for beds, no furniture of any kind, and at best a few rough implements for cooking and laundry. At one point he doubles back to snatch a discarded loincloth draped over a windowsill and knots it around his waist. The idea of killing a fellow human being while naked strikes him as somehow indecent.

He reaches the transverse lane that leads to the crossroads. He pushes on into the alley opposite, then turns right onto a narrow passageway that winds its way behind a crooked row of houses, picking his way through cramped, trash-strewn courtyards. When he senses that he is approaching the crossroads, he crouches down and proceeds at a crawl, his fist wrapped tightly around the cradle of the sling, which is already loaded. The main street leading from the gate is just ahead, but now he's north of the crossroads, so if he steps out into the open here and the dying soldier hasn't moved from where Hani found him yesterday, they will be face-to-face. Instead, he climbs through the window of the last hut in the row and flattens himself against the wall, just beside the front door. From here, he has a partial view down the street, but unless he leans out and reveals himself he can't see as far as the crossroads, which he estimates to be thirty cubits or so away, at most. At that distance, he ought to be able to get in one strong, accurate shot before the soldier is even aware that he's being stalked. He cranes his neck a little further and there they are — the feet in the buskins. He slides the middle finger of his right hand into the anchor loop and steps into the street, already beginning his windup.

The soldier is exactly as he left him, asleep with his legs splayed out before him and his head tilted to the right, his bare arms limp at his sides. Hani takes a brief moment to adjust his stance. The cord whistles sweetly as it spins behind his head, picking up speed and torque. Hani focuses his gaze on the soldier's forehead, steps into his swing, twists at the waist, snaps his wrist, and releases. The stone hits the parapet of the well with a muffled click, a hand's width to the left of the soldier's head — exactly where his forehead would have been if his head had been upright. The soldier starts and lifts his head but makes no further movement. He looks as if he has just woken from a deep sleep and has no idea where he is. His eyes scan the space before him, but it's not clear how much of it he can see. He certainly does not seem to have registered Hani's presence. Hani closes in at a trot.

They lock eyes only when Hani is right in front of him.

Like at their first meeting, the look on the soldier's face is impersonal, remote, mildly curious but detached, the way a very old person watches children at play. He doesn't look scared at all, nor does he duck or flinch when Hani bends over and slips the dagger from its scabbard. It's heavy, well-polished and oiled, made of the best iron, the most refined weapon Hani has ever held in his hands. It makes Hani's flint blade look like a child's toy. There will be no resistance when point meets flesh. Hani steps back, keeping his eye on the soldier, weighing his next move. It's obvious to him by now that his enemy is at the point of fatal collapse, barely able to focus his eyes, let alone defend himself. His lips are so swollen and cracked they look like oak bark. He's not sure how long a man can survive without water, but this one doesn't have long. He probably couldn't speak even if he wanted to, but he's showing no sign of having anything to say for himself. Up close, there's no way he's the Akhillisa or any kind of a ruthless killing machine. For one thing, they say the Akhillisa is a monster hideous to behold, and this man is young, smooth of skin, almost doe-eyed. Hani is free to do with him as he pleases. If he just leans in and nicks the artery in the soldier's neck, it will be all over in seconds, not a lot of blood, silent and painless for both of them. Maybe that's what he wants Hani to do. Hani himself might feel the same if he were in such a fix. He would probably be doing the soldier a favor, after all his lonely suffering so far from home. No one, no matter who they are, wants to die alone. In the company of a gentle and compassionate killer, you don't have to. Hani crouches down so that their eyes are level with one another, and they contemplate each other frankly. At last, Hani extends the dagger toward the man's chest, rests the point just above his heart. With a quick flick of the blade he severs the leather baldric and the scabbard drops into his outstretched hand. He stands up, sheathes the dagger, and walks, then runs off in the direction of the gate.

Back in the guardroom, he downs a swig of unmixed wine from the jug, then almost immediately brings it back up. He tries again with water, but his hands are still shaking uncontrollably. His bowels feel loose, his vision fuzzy. This is not what he wanted at all, or not what he had thought he wanted. It would have been so easy, and it would have made everything so simple. For Arinna's sake he should have killed him; he could still go back and kill him at any moment, although he knows he won't now. Is he a coward? Has he betrayed Arinna? Suddenly he feels a hot, churning hatred for the dying soldier for putting him in this impossible bind, but it's a helpless kind of hatred, the kind a little child feels when he's whacked on the back of the head by an adult for no reason. No, it's when the child knows there's a reason for his punishment, and a very good reason, that his humiliation and resentment are strongest. And that's what it is here. Hani knows exactly what he did wrong, and it would have been so easy to get it right, but he didn't.

Now, in any case, he can be quite sure the soldier is going

nowhere. If he leaves him be, he'll be dead in a day or two, at most. Hani has a lot of work to do, and every minute he does not spend looking for Arinna could be one minute too late. He does not have time to waste killing people of no consequence, and he could not care less whether the dying soldier is friend or foe. If that should change for any reason, Hani knows where to find him.

He returns to the barrier outside the city gate and plops himself down in its shadow, beside his belongings. He rummages through the knapsack, even though he knows exactly what's in there. Other than the few trinkets he has collected on his way, there is precisely one loaf of bread, as hard as a rock and probably beyond salvaging, and a bagful of barley that he has no way of cooking. So he knows what he must do first. It's been two days since he was last in the upper city, and the weather has remained relatively cool, so no matter what state of decay the corpses in the marketplace and the citadel might be in, he is going to have to take the chance of scavenging up there for anything that remains edible. If nothing else, the vegetables may still be in decent condition. And there's a whole maze of rooms in the palace that he has not yet explored; one of them is bound to contain provisions of some sort, if they haven't been pillaged.

The safest way to get there is to skirt the city wall, out in the open where he can see far in all directions, and re-enter via the destroyed west gate. But the fastest is to return to the crossroads where the soldier lies dying and to keep going until he reaches the market square, as he eventually must, as best he can tell, so that's what he does. He no longer believes that there are enemies skulking in the alleys, waiting to ambush him, but he keeps a sharp eye out and carries the dagger down low, by his thigh, in a tight fist. Every ten paces or so he calls out his sister's name. In the silence, it sounds like an accusation. When he reaches the crossroads, he casts a glance down the well and determines that it has not been polluted with bodies like those in the upper city. He bends down and shouts "Arinna!" right in the soldier's face, but even that provokes no reaction other than a subtle widening of the eyes.

Halfway up the street, he stops and turns and retraces his steps. He kneels before the soldier's feet and proceeds with the task he left unfinished the day before. As his hands busy themselves with the bootlaces, he and the dying soldier stare into one another's eyes. There's no way of knowing what the wounded man is thinking. It's like looking into the eyes of an animal, but he's not an animal so he must be thinking something. He must be thirsty and hungry, or maybe he's already past that. Does he hate Hani, either for stealing his boots or for failing to put him out of his misery? Hani would hate him if their places were reversed. Yet the dying soldier's gaze shows no sign of hatred, distress, anger, or any other emotion that Hani can identify. He looks thoughtful, the way a woodpecker examines the hole it's drilling, or the way a god might observe human activity from the vantage point of a window seat on Mount Hazzi. Just far off, and mildly interested. When Hani has slipped the buskins off his feet, he offers the dying soldier a terse "Thank you," and the soldier appears to nod, but that might be Hani's imagination. He waits until he's out of sight around a bend in the street before trying them on. They're too big, but they'll do until he can find some rags to wrap around his feet and make a better fit.

In the market square, the corpses have begun to smell. It's early yet, but there's definitely a sweet and rancid note in the air. Beetles and ants have begun their work around the deflated eyes and gaping mouths. Those bodies that are lying on their backs have bloated bellies, and one with his tunic hiked above his waist has a grotesquely swollen cock, like a horse's. Hani turns away and pretends to himself that he hasn't seen it. There's no sign of rats, vultures, or jackals, but they'll be here any minute. One good warm day will change everything. If Father or Arinna is here, and he's pretty sure they're not, this will definitely be Hani's last opportunity to identify them. They will not be recognizable once the scavengers get busy. The discs of cheese and strings of dried figs scattered across the pavement are crawling with ants, but he fills his bag with figs anyway, since the ants can always be washed off, as well as some onions and garlic. He promises himself that this will be his last visit to the upper city. If he doesn't find the provisions he needs, he will have to head back to the sea and figure out how to do some fishing.

The palace provides what he's looking for, and more. Of course, it's been thoroughly ransacked, but the invaders apparently had different ideas about what makes a thing valuable. Apparently, food didn't interest them. In the kitchen, he finds a clay pot that will be perfect for cooking his barley in, and in a low, vaulted chamber nearby there are sacks of horse beans, lentils, onions, dried chickpeas, wheat flour, and salt, as well as sealed jars of olive oil, wine, and honey. It's far more than he can bring with him, but after packing what he can carry on his back, he hauls the rest to the citadel ramparts and lowers it all to the ground on the far side in a basket at the end of a length of rope he has found. Now, when his provisions have been exhausted, he will be able to replenish them without having to go all the way back to the upper city. Before leaving the palace, he returns to the decorated walls of the dining hall. He sits cross-legged on the floor and drinks his fill of the scenes depicted there. He's especially taken with the farming scenes, as if the person who painted them had paid him a very personal and thoughtful compliment. He tries to memorize it all so that he'll be able to picture the wall with his eyes closed for the rest of his life.

At the bottom of the citadel ramp, he turns left to explore the upper city neighborhoods that he has not yet visited. The residences here are more substantial than those in the lower city, tall and broad and made of brick and stone instead of mud. They must have driven the pillagers crazy with rage. Most have been sacked and burned; all are scorched shells, though many of their walls still stand. There's nothing here worth scavenging. As he follows the downward slope of the neighborhood, he calls Arinna's name again and again. When she doesn't respond, he tries singing "Here Child" — the secret song for reuniting animal and human mothers with their lost babies — but he can't remember the words in any language. Here, where the streets are wider and more open to the sky than in the lower city, his voice sounds weak and woebegone, like that of a hungry fledgling in a nest.

He returns to the lower city, taking a roundabout route. He has decided that even though the guardroom is only three minutes from the well where the dying soldier lies, it's too comfortable and convenient to abandon. He leaves all his newfound provisions there, then gathers the rest of his belongings from the barrier and moves them to his new home. By the time he's collected a sizable stockpile of firewood from the abandoned shanties nearby, it's early evening and he's hungry. He grabs his waterskins and sets off for the well.

For the sake of varying his route in case he's being watched, he approaches the well from the west. This gives him a good view of the dying soldier in profile. Even asleep and in his reduced state he's a noble-looking man, maybe in his late teens or early twenties, although Hani is not very good at guessing ages. He has a fine, straight nose and sharp jawline, and even after all these days lying in the dirt in a plundered city, his braids are tight and symmetrical under their coating of lime dust. His beard is patchy and almost colorless, so he may be even younger than he looks. Hani is convinced he must be from a highborn family; a common man would never submit to this kind of death and shame with such dignity. Hani is grateful to himself that he decided not to kill the dying soldier, as it might come across as impertinent for someone like him to do violence to someone like that. There are very few circumstances in which it's acceptable for a poor man to strike or kill a rich one. Hani can appreciate that. The dying soldier might take it as the ultimate humiliation, and it could even upset his journey to the underworld.

There's a length of hemp twine tied to a stake drilled into the stone of the parapet, and at its other end is a leather bucket with which he draws bright clean water from the well. Hani plunges a waterskin into the bucket and holds it down as it fills, sending a froth of bubbles to the surface. As it fills, Hani glances down at the dying soldier and is surprised to see his eyes focused intently on the bucket. The gurgling of the bubbles appears to have awakened him, as if someone has called his name. His gaze is lively, keen. This is another indication of his noble birth—a poor man has less to live for than a rich one and would not have hung on to life nearly so long as this. It's an impressive performance, if pointless. The dying soldier shifts his gaze from the bucket to Hani and then back again. It seems to take every ounce of his remaining energy, and he shudders and closes his eyes.

His stubbornness reminds Hani of a ewe from the valley that gave birth to four lambs over the course of an entire night of laboring in a howling gale, and how she refused to die until all four were safely delivered. Hani attended the lambing himself and remembers it well. No one had ever seen such stout nobility in a sheep before. Everyone in the valley talked about her silent courage and endurance the next day. All four lambs died, of course, but that wasn't the point. The ewe, like the dying soldier, had exhibited rare resolve in a moment of crisis. Hani thinks about it all evening as he eats his chickpeas and onions and drinks wine mellowed with honey and fresh water.

Before going to sleep, he plays a full round of under-the-arch with the knucklebones, just to keep his skills in tune. He often plays by himself when there's no one around to compete against, but tonight the game feels forced and lifeless and he has to chide himself into playing all the way to the end.

That night, he awakens from a dream in which he revisited the winter lambing and saw himself dabbing water on the dying ewe's lips with a wet rag. Arinna was also in there somewhere. Was she actually present or was she more like a presiding spirit, the way you can smell the rain falling on the hills many leagues away? Hani can't remember. She might have been the ewe but she might also have been the lamb asking to be born. Either one would have made sense.

The next morning, he hurries to the well, afraid to find

that he's too late. On previous encounters, the dying soldier opened his eyes at Hani's approach; this time, Hani has to prod him with his toe, first gently then forcefully, to get him to wake up. When he does, he doesn't know where he is; he can't focus his eyes and doesn't seem to see Hani at all, or anything really. Hani uses the edge of his loincloth, dipped in the bucket, to dampen his cracked lips. The soldier closes his eyes but otherwise does not react. Hani tries it again, and again, until finally the soldier licks his lips. They do this a few more times until Hani squeezes a few drops of water from the cloth onto the soldier's outstretched tongue. He knows not to do more than that right away, as the soldier's stomach will only cramp.

He examines the soldier's wound. It's angry and red along its entire length, swollen and dripping with pus. It has also begun to smell. When Hani cleans it, he can see black and green in there, spongy and stringy. This will kill him soon, for sure. Hani washes the soldier's face, neck, arms, and hands. The soldier does not open his eyes. Hani tries using his finger to push a clot of mashed chickpeas past the soldier's teeth, but it doesn't take. Instead, he again moistens the soldier's lips until he sticks out his tongue, on which Hani dabs a light smear of honey. With his own teeth, Hani tears a scrap of fabric from the loincloth, soaks it in the water, and leaves it draped over the soldier's hand, within reach of the bucket.

He is at Ansa's cairn twenty minutes later. He's relieved

to see it undisturbed, as he's well aware how clever hungry scavengers can be when put to the test. He greets her gently and tells her how much he misses her and apologizes for the inadequacy of her grave. He remembers precisely how her body is oriented and begins to remove the stones closest to her forelegs, one by one. It does not take long to uncover her front hooves. The left one is a little discolored but otherwise unchanged, but the right one, where she was injured, is pulsing with maggots. Begging her forgiveness, and whispering in soothing tones of his love for her, he saws at the hoof below the fetlock. The dagger is as razor sharp as a soldier's weapon should be, but it takes more time and effort than he anticipated. He cuts through the hide and two ropy tendons, then tries to separate the hoof from the leg by wedging the blade between the bones of the pastern. When that doesn't work, he smashes the bones with a rock until they are crushed and the hoof comes away. He cradles it in his hands, careful to disturb as few maggots as he can, and lowers it gingerly into the knapsack. He replaces the stones above Ansa's forelegs and says a brief prayer.

At the well, the dying soldier has not touched the wet rag that Hani left for him, but when Hani drips water onto his lips he opens his mouth like a nestling. Hani crouches at his feet and retrieves the severed hoof from the sack. Holding the hoof above the soldier's wounded leg, he begins to gently nudge the maggots directly into the wound and does not stop until every last one has been transferred from the hoof.

He turns the sack inside out and shakes every stray maggot onto the leg. Almost immediately, the maggots reorient themselves to their new home, quivering with revived appetite, and set about their business. Hani has seen this operation performed many times by farmers tending to wounded livestock, and he knows how to do it. Fashioning a bandage from his loincloth, he wraps the injured leg from groin to knee. Protected and undisturbed, the maggots should work their magic within the next forty-eight hours. If the pollution has not traveled to the blood, the soldier will survive.

When he has tied off the dressing, he glances up to find the soldier watching him. His expression, as always, is impossible to read. Has he been monitoring the entire procedure? If so, it ought to be a look of horror. Animals have no problem with maggots, but people are revolted by them for some reason. When Tudha's father tried the maggot trick on his sister after she broke her leg falling down a ravine and went missing for four days, his mother was so horrified and disgusted that she refused to allow him to do it, and the sister died. Hani is absolutely sure that the soldier will die, too, if he prevents the maggots from doing their work. He may die either way; it's amazing that he's lived as long as he has. But he doesn't look horrified. If Hani had to guess, he'd say it was a look of mellow interest, and maybe gratitude, but that could just be his own imagination at work. He raises the nipple of the waterskin to the soldier's lips, and now the soldier drinks. After a few moments, Hani pulls the waterskin away, and the soldier seems to understand that this is for his own good. Hani dips his finger into the bowl of mashed chick-peas, now cold and muddy, and comes away with a pea-sized lump, which he balances on the soldier's lower lip. The sol-dier licks it off. They do this again and again until the soldier has eaten enough for his first meal in days, but not so much as to make him sick. He falls asleep as soon as it becomes clear that he is not getting any more.

Hani roams the abandoned homes of the lower city until he finds a length of threadbare fabric to replace the loincloth. Now that he knows he's no longer the only person left alive in the world, not counting Arinna, he's resigned to going back to the practice of covering himself. He was very happy to go naked when he thought there was no one left to see him, but that's all over now. We all of us live among people, even if it's only one of them, and we are none of us free to make these decisions for ourselves. It's a minor sacrifice and inconvenience, but it also means you don't have to look at other people in their nakedness and shame. Just think of all those people up the hill who died without their clothes on. Hani knows full well that every one of them is wishing he had Hani's loincloth to cover himself right this minute.

HIS FATHER USED TO tell him — often while administering a beating — that every time you make a decision you change the future. Hani knew full well that what Father meant was that he could avoid the next drubbing by choosing to behave in a particular way, but when Hani first heard it, at the age of six or seven, his head spun with the possibilities. He tried out the line on all his friends, who were equally excited by its bold challenge. I can change the future? You can change the future. We can change the future! You can't do anything about the past because what happened happened and can't be unhappened, but the future can be one thing one minute and another thing the next, and all you have to do is decide what you want to make of it. You are the master of time! This idea felt so exhilarating to Hani and Tudha and Alak that they spent weeks running around the farm changing the future with a wave of the hand and competing with one another to change it fastest and most. *Most* meant a complete reversal of the future, like if you said, "I'm going to swim in the river" and a minute later you said, "I'm *not* going to swim in the river." "I will marry Kanza—I will *not* marry Kanza." "I will kill the Akhillisa with my bare hands—the Akhillisa will kill you with his little toe!" With one brief sentence you could turn the future on its head. It took Hani's gang some time to figure out that no matter how many times you changed the future, you always ended up with just one future, and that one was just as dull and boring as any of the other futures. It was like playing catch with a hard-boiled egg.

But Hani's recent experience has caused him to see things differently. He has begun to think lately that in its own way the past is just as changeable as the future. It's true, some-times you do something that can't be undone. If you build a house it stays built, and every time you walk by it, it stands as proof of something you did in the past, and that doesn't change no matter how you look at it. If you catch a frog and eat it, that frog stays caught and eaten forever. But mostly, the only proof you have of something you once did is how you see it now, and that never stays the same. You're really hungry, so the frog tastes delicious, but when you remember it later you think it tasted only so-so, and if you think about it after you've eaten a honey cake it tasted disgusting. So the taste of the frog keeps changing even though you only ate it one time. You move on, you go forward, and every time you look back you're seeing the past from a new perspective. When Hani and Ansa walked from the valley to the city, there was a mountain on the southern horizon that changed every time they looked at it, because they were always seeing it from a different vantage point. Hani knew—or maybe Ansa knew, and Hani suspected—that the mountain wasn't really changing shape or growing bigger or shrinking, but he had no proof of that. If he relied just on the evidence of his eyes, which have never let him down, he'd have to admit that the mountain was as restless as a cloud. The past changes just like the future, and you can never be sure that the thing you remember is the thing as it was when you saw it or the thing as it is now. Did you think that or did you think this? Did he say this or did he say that? Was she like this or was she like that?

Arinna is his sister and she will always be his sister. He is the one who is responsible for her safety and well-being, and he will always be the one. But everything else is beginning to change, to melt at the edges. Going from house to house these past few days, inspecting each one inside out before moving on to the next, he's had lots of time to think about her, about who she really is. The search itself has been easy enough; most of the houses have only one room, or two at most, like his family home in the valley. None so far has yielded any big surprises, except for an occasional grandma left to die in her bed, or a little child's toy, a horse or a spinning top, forlornly guarding a barren patch of kingdom. But conjuring Arinna has proved a little more complicated. He continues to call out her name, but both the name and the language are sounding less and less familiar to him, more mismatched, as if maybe somehow they no longer fit her, like a dress she's growing out of and thinking of handing down to a younger friend. He keeps worrying, and then scolding himself for worrying, that she won't respond to it, as if there were another Hani out there calling for a different Arinna. He knows it's stupid but even so he's finding it harder and harder to picture the Arinna for whom the name was a perfect fit. She has changed — not the Arinna who is, if she still is, but the Arinna who was, the one he knew back home, the one he saw and loved every day of his life. It's not that he can't remember her — he can reconstruct her face precisely in his mind's eye, he knows exactly where the top of her head comes to on his shoulder, he can hear her piping voice just as clearly as he hears his own. What he can't do is match that person with the one he loves, the one he has come all this way to find. The strange and confusing thing is, the Arinna who is here in the city somewhere, waiting for him to find her, is the one he knows. It's the one he left behind that has changed. She has shed her body and become a kind of living spirit. He's confident that this will all come together when he finds her, like when you dive into the river and your face and its reflection meet on the surface of the water, but in the meantime it's worrisome and annoying. The person he's

looking for—the person he tells himself he's looking for—
is a little girl, with hair and eyes and breath, not a ghost.

Determined to keep Arinna front and center of his mission, he has avoided visiting the dying soldier these past two
days. The last time he saw him, Hani left him with the wine
jug, full of water, as well as one of the waterskins. He was
pretty confident that the dying soldier had enough strength
to lift the jug to his lips, and that by the time he drained
it he would be strong enough to lift the skin, which is a
lot heavier. He also left him the large pot, filled with barley gruel seasoned with salt and honey, and a broken cup he
had found earlier, in lieu of a spoon. As for his wound, in
Hani's experience it should take the maggots two to three
days to do their work. If they do it right, the wound should
be clean and free of corruption upon Hani's return. If not,
he'll offer a quick prayer, collect his jug and waterskin, and
be on his way.

In the meanwhile, he has completed a full sweep of the
houses of the lower city. Now that he knows the city's streets
fairly well, he has come to believe that the invaders breached
its defenses through the south and west gates, both of which
face the bay. It looks like someone may have opened the
south gate to them from the inside. From there, they herded
the terrified citizens to the market neighborhood, where they
separated the women and children, then boxed in all who
remained and slaughtered them so there would be no enemy

at their backs when they stormed the citadel. He wondered about all those dead people, who they were, what their lives were like. He wasn't sure how to feel about them. On the bad side, they had all lived crammed together in tiny houses on dark, narrow, and filthy streets, corralled inside walls that couldn't even keep them safe in the end. What a dim, vain, and dreary life they must have led. He thinks they probably spoke the same language he does, or something like it, and that they must have worshipped the same gods and worn the same sort of clothes, but the way they lived was completely foreign and incomprehensible. Why would anyone want to live this way? On the good side, Hani can tell just by looking at the way their houses are set up that they had families like his, so they must have had the same kind of home life, too. They must have often worked side by side and eaten together and gone hungry together, yelled at each other and sometimes laughed at each other's jokes; they must have lain awake at night and whispered and listened to each other snore and dream. There must have been mothers who died in childbirth and the bewildered kids they left behind, who kept making the same mistakes because they didn't have anybody to teach them any better. And those kids, some of whom must have been the same age as Hani and Arinna, had grown up knowing nothing but war and hardship and fear, too, or probably worse, since the war was literally at their doorstep.

Now that he has failed to locate Arinna in the lower city,

he will have to turn his attention to the wealthier districts up the hill. He has a lot less imagination for the lives of rich folk, the way they talk to each other and treat each other when there are no poor people around. He imagines they must be lazy and stupid and bossy, but he has to admit he could be wrong, he really doesn't know anything about the rich or how they think. He's seen one or two at a distance but he's never actually met any of them, although the dying soldier is probably a nobleman of some sort, and there's nothing bossy about him. It's just that if Hani lived in one of those great big houses with all those rooms and courtyards, those whispering gardens and burbling fountains, he might be less willing to allow himself to be driven from his home by some barbarian invader. He might be more motivated to stay and fight for what is his. Hani hopes that's not the case; he hopes that the rich, like the poor, allowed themselves to be chased out of their houses and herded like cattle before being cut down in the streets like everyone else. Because if the rich stood their ground and defended their homes, there will be dead people piled up in every room in every house, and his search for Arinna is going to turn really nasty. The stench of death already hangs over the upper city like a green cloud and is detectable even at the south gate, and he's likely to run into legions of jackals and rats half-drunk and delirious on a diet of ripe carrion. This is a good time to be wearing sturdy buskins.

House-to-house scouting is hot work in these close

streets, especially now that the weather is turning. Spring has just about run its course, and the blue skies over the sea have begun to pile up with moody cloud mountains in the midafternoon. Hani goes down to the river to bathe. He'd like to return to the sea sometime and have another leisurely swim in that lovely warm water, but it's a long walk and there's so much else to do and not a lot of time to do it in. Still, the river is cold and clear and reminds him of his river at home; it's a different kind of comfort but it does the trick. There where it widens near the ford, carp gather in the shallows to face upstream. He's sure they would taste good and promises that he will return for them tomorrow, even if he has to catch them with his bare hands. On his walk back to the gatehouse, there's still just enough strength left in the ebbing breeze to dry his body and hum a faint song in his ear.

He can see the soldier's legs as he approaches the well from the gatehouse. The soldier has not moved from the position he occupied when Hani first stumbled upon him four days earlier. Hani assumes with a sinking heart that he must be dead, as no living man can sit in the same position all that time without developing sores and cramps. But when he rounds the well he finds that the soldier is not dead. Far from it, he lifts and turns his head at the sound of Hani's footsteps and even attempts a tentative smile. The jug is empty and the waterskin flaccid. When Hani bends over to peer into the clay pot, the soldier picks it up and holds it out for his inspection. Most of the gruel is gone. Hani holds the dagger down below his left thigh, where the soldier can't see it, and cocks his head as he considers the injured man. The color has returned to his cheeks and his expression is brighter, if still opaque. There's no reason in the world for Hani to trust him.

"Why don't you say something?" he asks.

He goes down on one knee and begins to unwrap the dressing from the soldier's wounded thigh, taking care to keep the dagger within easy reach. He places the palm of his hand underneath the left knee and lifts it until the sole of the left foot is flat on the ground, then begins to slowly unwind the bandage. He holds his breath, in case the stink of putrefaction has intensified, but there's no smell to speak of. The innermost layer of the dressing is stained green and yellow, but when he tugs it gently, it falls away without sticking. A cascade of fat white maggots, each one five times bigger than it was two days ago, falls from the wound onto the ground. They immediately begin to inch blindly away in all directions. Those that remain in the wound writhe and thrash as they seek shelter from the daylight, but they have consumed every loose flap and fold of dead flesh and there's nowhere left for them to hide. Hani splashes them off with a jet from the waterskin, and the wound is fully revealed. It's as deep as the first knuckle of his thumb and longer than an outstretched hand, but all the discoloration is gone, leaving it bright pink. The dying soldier will carry an ugly scar for the rest of his life, but he'll live, for now at any rate. Hani washes the loincloth and leaves it to dry on the parapet of the well. He steps away and returns the dagger to its sheath, which is hanging against his back. From a safe distance, he considers the dying soldier, who is probably not dying anymore, and what he should do about him.

"Don't they talk where you're from?"

Hani's mother once told him that when you save someone's life you are responsible for him forever. He can't remember the incident connected with this lesson and he was pretty young when it happened, but it has always stuck with him, maybe because he has three dead brothers. He's already responsible for Arinna, but he will be even more so when he finds her and saves her. Now he supposes he's responsible for the soldier, too. He certainly didn't start out wanting to save him, but somehow it happened and it can't be undone or denied. He could have killed him, or walked away, but instead he gave him water when he was thirsty and food when he was hungry and tended to him when he was sick, so there really isn't any way around it at this point. If he walks away from him now, it will be as if he had never helped him, or worse, since the dying soldier was already well past halfway dead when Hani found him and now he'd have to start dying all over again. Hani doesn't even know if the soldier is a friend or an enemy. If he's an enemy maybe he will just wait patiently until Hani has restored him to full health and then take back his dagger and slit his throat, which enemies seem to enjoy and are good at, but if Hani is responsible for him that's a chance he'll have to take, and he's beginning to think the soldier isn't that kind of enemy anyway.

Hani replenishes the jug from the well, then empties and washes the pot and returns with it to the gatehouse. He half fills it with lentils, chops up an onion, and mixes it all with water and salt, then leaves it to simmer on a fire that he has kept burning just outside the gatehouse door, banking it at night to conceal his presence from wandering eyes. While the lentils are cooking, he rummages through his rucksack to retrieve his treasures, which he sets out on the floor, side by side, in the order in which he found them. Here is the amulet discovered on the road to the city. Next is the onyx ring borrowed from the corpse trapped in the gateway, then the green gemstone brooch from the palace. Last is the clay tablet swiped from the storage room, covered in the same cryptic markings as the amulet. Each is precious and unique in its own way, each unlike anything Hani has ever seen, let alone possessed. Any of them would make a prized gift. The question is, which one? He carefully assesses each in turn.

Back at the well, he squats down before the soldier, knees splayed, rests the fingertips of both hands on his own chest, and says, "Hani." His meaning could not be clearer. This is exactly the way he would introduce himself to a stranger from the neighboring valley. A dog would get it. There isn't a human being in the world who wouldn't understand that he's sharing the secret of his own name. But the soldier just stares at him blankly, so Hani does it again, and this time, after touching his own chest, he flips his hands over and offers the soldier his palms, meaning *I've just given you something precious. Now you must give me something precious in return.* The soldier smiles and cocks his head a bit but says nothing. His eyes are not saying *I understand that you're asking something of me but I don't know what it is.* Nor are they saying *I know what you want but I have no intention of giving it to you.* Instead, they seem to be saying something like *This is fun. Do it again,* like a dog waiting for a stick to be thrown, which is confusing. Hani hadn't taken him for a simpleton, and he doesn't do so now. So what then?

"I am Hantili," he says forcefully, assuming that the soldier is more likely to understand him if he speaks louder. "Who are you?" He points to his own mouth and then to the soldier's, but the soldier just shakes his head. That could mean anything. Hani grasps his own chin and pretends to yank his own mouth open, and the soldier copies him. Hani peers into his mouth. The soldier's tongue is intact and healthy, and he does not appear to have any injuries to his palate or throat. Hani is sure the soldier understands him, so the fact that he doesn't answer is no proof that they speak different languages. Nor does he believe that the soldier is deliberately holding back because he doesn't want to reveal anything of himself, the way a prisoner of war might refuse to be interrogated. The problem is, now that Hani has revealed himself, the soldier knows if they are on the same side or on opposite sides, but Hani does not. It's to the soldier's advantage not to say anything, at least until he's recovered enough to defend himself or attack. On the other hand, he's not acting like someone with violence on his mind. He smiles, accepts Hani's help, and shows no fear. Why would a friend who knows how to speak refuse to say so much as "hello" to another friend?

Hani can only conclude that, unless he was born mute, the soldier just doesn't want to talk.

In Hani's experience, people usually don't talk to each other when they think they won't be understood. Children clam up around grown-ups because they know the grown-ups won't understand them. Grown-ups don't talk about certain things around children for the same reason. Parents having an argument eventually stop talking to each other when they can't make themselves understood. Maybe the soldier isn't talking because he knows Hani won't understand what he has to say. That could be because he speaks a different language, or because he thinks he's smarter than Hani, or because he's not as smart as he thinks he is, or because he is the Akhillisa, or because he's a god, or because he has a secret never to be told, or because he has lost someone dear to him and believes that no one can share his grief, or because he was dropped on his head as a baby, or for some other reason — for many other reasons, most of them sinister or murky.

Hani gets up and crosses the lane to sit with his back against the wall of the house opposite. He and the soldier eye one another mildly for a while, Hani as unable to snatch a coherent meaning from his own thoughts as he is from the soldier's. Technically, since the soldier is now disarmed and can neither run away nor attend to his own needs, he's Hani's captive, yet Hani suspects that he's more afraid of the soldier than the soldier is of him. He's afraid of the soldier and yet he feels warmly toward him, is drawn to him and wants to help him, as if he were a wise, wayward uncle who has returned to the fold. It's irritating to find himself so turned around by these jostling instincts, for which his quiet life in the valley has left him ill-prepared. As always, Arinna would know what to do, because feeling two different things at the same time doesn't scare her the way it scares most people, including Hani. He breaks out the knucklebones and plays stables, solo, to focus his mind. The soldier eyes him with baffling detachment, then falls asleep.

At the gatehouse, the lentils are ready. He molds two flat loaves of bread out of flour, oil, salt, and water and bakes them on a roof tile set directly into the embers. He returns to the well and serves the soldier his dinner. The soldier eats heartily from the pot, Hani from a cracked bowl he salvaged the day before. They mop up the leavings with the last scraps of bread. When they're done, Hani reaches into the knucklebone pouch and pulls out the amulet and the tablet and hands them to the soldier, who examines each one closely, turning it over in his palm again and again. He frowns as his eyes scan the markings minutely, darting restlessly back and forth like a trout caught in a net. But then at last he sighs and shakes his head. Hani is surprised—he was convinced that a man as worldly and cultured as the soldier seems to be would just naturally understand what the markings meant, but even he is stumped. The soldier returns the items to Hani with a shrug, and Hani restores them to the pouch.

That night, kept awake by his perplexity over the mysterious convalescent, Hani makes a decision. So long as the soldier refuses to speak, he too will hold his tongue and say no more. Whatever the two of them have to say to one another, they can do it in gestures or pantomime. That, at any rate, will help maintain the delicate balance of power between them that Hani upset when he became the first to speak. Hani will nurse him in silence until he's able to fend for himself, and then they will go their separate ways, knowing no more about one another than they absolutely need to know for their own survival.

But the next morning, when Hani arrives at the well with fresh water and a round of bread, the soldier is animated and agitated and ignores his breakfast. He repeatedly jabs his finger vigorously into the air toward Hani and then toward his own chest, back and forth again and again until Hani grasps his meaning.

"You want to know my name? It's Hantili. Han-ti-li. Hani."

The soldier nods excitedly and beckons Hani to his side. He smooths out a circle in the dust with the palm of his hand and begins to draw shapes in it with his index finger. The first looks like a trident or a fork. The second looks like a fishing hook, the third like a tree in fruit. The last vaguely resembles a skirt blowing in the wind, or maybe a river flowing through a valley. Hani studies the images and shrugs.

"Okay. What?"

The soldier stares at him and knits his eyebrows, impatiently erases the shapes, then draws them again, exactly the same. Their meaning is no clearer to Hani now than they were the first time. The soldier again stares at him as if he were an idiot. Hani has never been accused of being an idiot and is not at all used to thinking of himself as an idiot, but he's at a complete loss to understand what is expected of him. The soldier keeps poking at his own chest, then pointing at the drawings, but it isn't helping.

"Fork. Hook. Tree. River. I don't get it."

Exasperated, the soldier changes tack and stabs repeatedly at Hani with his forefinger.

"Me. What? Me? Hani?"

The soldier nods, then immediately draws a sun and a fruit tree beneath the four original drawings. He points at Hani, then at the new drawings. Hani frowns, squints, cocks his head.

"That's me? I'm a sun and a tree? Hani? How am I a sun and a tree?"

Again and again, he points first at Hani then back at the two drawings, jabbing at each in turn, and Hani repeats his name while the soldier nods, then holds up his palm as if telling him to stop. What does he want? He's egging him on with one gesture and silencing him with the other. Or slowing him down?

"Ha? Ni?"

The soldier smiles and nods vigorously. He says it again. When he says "ha," the soldier points to the sun. When he says "ni," the soldier points to the tree.

"So the sun means 'ha' and the tree means 'ni'? Ha. Ni. Ha-ni. The picture isn't a thing. It's a sound?"

The soldier smiles again, points at himself and then at the four original drawings.

"So that means you? It's your name, four sounds. Okay. Four sounds, one of them is 'ni.' Something, something, ni, something."

And it's at this moment that he realizes that the soldier has again tricked him into revealing something about himself without offering anything in return. Without saying another word or even a backward glance, he gets up and leaves.

He spends the rest of the day angrily roaming the alleys and homes of the upper city and calling out Arinna's name. He avoids the major arteries where the corpses lie piled up, although he can smell them now wherever he goes, forceful but not yet overwhelming, and it confirms his resolve to steer clear of them. As much as he wants to concentrate on his search and set all other distractions aside, he can't shake his annoyance at having allowed himself to be sucked into the soldier's game, whatever he's playing at with his little sound pictures. It's not safe in this strange place to be so trusting and forthcoming—not safe for himself and not safe for Arinna. He's spent so much time alone these past weeks, and been so pleased to exercise survival skills he didn't even know he had, that he's almost forgotten that he's still a child—not too far from manhood, maybe, but hardly equipped to defend himself against a grown man trained in warfare, let alone whatever else may be lying in wait around any corner, no matter how cocky he might feel with an iron dagger in his hand. This is not the time or the place to be learning lessons the hard way.

But as the hot day drags on he finds himself drawn back again and again to the pictures in the dust and the mystery wrapped up inside them. He knows what they are. They look nothing like the scratchy tangle of lines on his amulet, but they must do the same thing in a different way. It comes as no surprise that someone like the soldier, with his soft hands and expressive face, would know how to use them. Since he first heard about this magic when he was little, Hani has believed in it, known in his heart that it must exist because it makes such simple sense and solves such a simple problem, but he has never expected to come into such close contact with it, let alone have someone try to teach it to him. He's not really sure what it's good for—after all, if someone wants to know his name they only have to ask—but he's absolutely sure, he knows, that it's a gateway to something completely new and unexpected. It's another kind of secret language, it has the same power and mystery, and the soldier wants to teach it to him.

And now that Hani has learned two of the drawings himself, has a little of their magic leaked into him? He can scratch his name on a stone and it will still say *Hani* for all to see ten, a hundred, a thousand years from now. It will be as if the future itself were set in that stone, unchanging forever, and in the future everyone will know that there was once a boy named Hani and maybe they will ask themselves who he was and what he did, if he was good at knucklebones or slinging shot, like a king in a burial mound only better. It's a secret language with one big advantage — it doesn't collapse when one of the people who knows it goes away.

Taking a water break in the shade of a crumbling wall, he scratches out his sun and his tree in the dust again and again, repeating their sounds over and over. He has heard his name spoken countless times, by all kinds of people in every possible tone of voice, but it sounds different when it radiates from these symbols in the dirt. It sounds like an incantation, like a prayer. Like a song. Before he leaves to pursue his quest, he scratches the sun and the tree into the red clay of the brick wall, then stands back to admire it. *Hani was here*, it says. High overhead, vultures wheel with abiding intent.

That evening, he arrives at the well bearing a gift. The soldier's eyes widen when he sees the brocaded robe, and widen further still when Hani unfolds it on the ground at his side and helps him inch and shuffle his way onto it. He hisses in pain and his face turns red when he shifts his injured leg, but he's a soldier and masters himself like one. When the transfer is complete, there's enough loose fabric at the top to drape around his shoulders, and this makes him look more like the aristocrat he is. He wears it comfortably and, Hani thinks, with gratitude. After they have polished off a pot of beans, Hani gets down to work. He prepares a broad circle of cleared dust within reach of the soldier's right hand.

"Arinna," he says, glancing meaningfully at the ground. "A–ri–na."

The soldier nods solemnly and proceeds to draw a kind of draft-pole, a man with his arms outstretched and his hair blowing in the wind, and a plowshare. When he's done, he points to each drawing in turn as Hani sounds them out. Hani does not tell him why he wants to know and the soldier does not ask. When it's his turn, the soldier erases Arinna and restores the four drawings of his own name. They start with the first and Hani goes through every possible sound a human mouth can make until the trident is identified as the sound *re.* They start all over again with the fishhook. They already know the tree sound, so they move straight on to the river. When it's over, and the night has all but fallen about them, Hani knows the soldier's name.

"Rewonida? Seriously? That's your name? Rewonida? What kind of a name is Rewonida?"

The soldier laughs silently and waggles his head, which Hani takes to mean that it's not really Rewonida but close enough. And then the light fails and Hani is forced to find his way to the gatehouse by grazing his fingers along the walls of the houses lining the street. In the upper city, jackals howl like abandoned children, their sobs bouncing off the citadel ramparts. Bereft of his robe and reduced to his scratchy old wool blanket, Hani falls asleep to visions of the land of Rewonidas and its handsome, gallant masters.

He sets off for the river before dawn with the dagger bound to a scorched pole that he has pillaged, along with a couple of bronze oil lamps, from the wreckage of a rich man's palace. The fish don't know what's hit them; he spears four fat carp in the time it takes to spot them and take aim. He would take more but they are lazy and plentiful and will surely be waiting for him in the same place tomorrow. Back at the gatehouse, he guts them, skewers them on the pole, and spit-roasts them. They make a fine breakfast with hot bread and cold water, the first flesh he has tasted since the last of the frog legs. The soldier enjoys his with equal relish.

The soldier thinks they are friends now and wants to pursue their lessons, but Hani remains wary, despite their breakthrough. He imagines that, in his mind, the soldier addresses him as *Hani,* but he can't think of the soldier as *Rewonida.* It's such a stupid name, bumbling, a toddler's name for an imaginary friend, like trying to tell a joke with your mouth full of pebbles. But it's also a threshold of intimacy that he's not sure he's ready to cross. When somebody calls you by your name it means they think they know something about you; it's like a spell that works only on you. When you return the favor, you're accepting their version of the story. It makes you look weak, and looking weak can be the same as being weak and can lead to mistakes. Hani has no idea if this is really true or not, but it sounds clever. It sounds like the kind of wisdom someone with deep experience in self-preservation and the treachery of men might share—not someone like Hani, whose first impulse is always to make friends and trust strangers.

So instead of playing with drawings, he stands before the soldier and gestures for him to get up. He has been sitting here by the well for too long now; if he doesn't start stretching his limbs and exercising his injured leg, his muscles will seize and he may never be able to walk or run properly again. Plus, now that he's eating again he's going to have to empty his bowels soon. Hani is actually a little surprised that the soldier has made no effort at all to get back on his feet—as a military man he should understand what's at stake—but since he hasn't Hani is going to do it for him. At first the soldier pretends he doesn't know what Hani is asking him to do, but that's hard to keep up for long and he begins to shake his head vehemently, with a look almost of fear in his eyes.

"Don't be a baby," Hani scolds. The soldier may not understand his words, but his meaning is clear. "Shame on you. A warrior shouldn't be scared of a little pain."

But the soldier absolutely refuses to cooperate, even when Hani offers to help him up by the elbow, and since he's twice

Hani's size there's nothing Hani can do to force the matter. Hani abandons the mission in disgust and heads to the upper city to continue his search. He supposes the soldier must resent his moodiness in some way, and that somewhere in the back of his mind he may worry that Hani will abandon him. Since he has heard Hani calling out for Arinna, and since the first thing Hani asked to learn in the magic drawings was her name, the soldier must understand by now that he's searching for someone dear to him. If he were the soldier, Hani would be nervous of being abandoned and left to starve to death or torn apart by slavering jackals whenever that search came to an end. Hani is inclined to feel a little guilty for leaving the soldier with that impression, but maybe it's a good thing. Maybe it will push him to begin learning how to fend for himself again, if he can. Especially since there's precious little left of the city that Hani has not explored. If Hani were the soldier, he'd be worried about what happens if Arinna is nowhere to be found.

Even so, when Hani happens upon a sturdy staff in the course of his afternoon rounds, it immediately puts him in mind of a new opportunity. Back at the gatehouse, he uses the dagger to split the staff down half its length, then stuffs the gap with a length of old cloth in such a way that it protrudes from the top, like a mushroom on a skewer. When he brings the soldier his dinner, he performs a demonstration of the use of the crutch, parading back and forth with a grotesquely exaggerated limp until the soldier is doubled over in silent laughter. When Hani extends his hand, the soldier shakes his head but grasps at Hani's wrist. Hani is not strong enough to pull him to his feet, but together they somehow manage to seat the soldier on the edge of the parapet. He closes his eyes and clamps his hands on either side of his wounded thigh, humming and bobbing up and down like a priest in prayer.

While he recovers, Hani busies himself removing the buskins from his own feet and ever so gently slipping them onto the soldier's feet and lacing them around his calves. The soldier watches the process intently, wincing. When his pain appears to subside, he takes in a deep, sharp breath and lets it out slowly. Then he looks up and nods gamely to Hani, who loops his left arm around the soldier's back, helps him to his feet, and relays the crutch to his left hand. The soldier jams the crutch under his left armpit and sways, reaching out to steady himself on Hani's shoulder. He's as shaky on his feet as a newborn foal. It's only now that Hani registers the appalling stink rising from him and his bloodstained tunic. When the soldier is able to stay upright without assistance, Hani mimes for him to wait and reaches for the dagger and uses it to make a nick in the neckline of the tunic. He clasps the two sides of the rip in his fists and slowly pulls them apart until the tunic is neatly torn from hem to hem and falls away, leaving the soldier naked. Hani raises a bucket of water from the well and hops up on the parapet, positioning himself directly above and behind the soldier. They both know how cold this water is, so while the soldier braces himself, Hani tips the bucket by tiny degrees until the first trickle lands in the dead center of the crown of the soldier's head. Despite having prepared himself, the soldier startles and wavers but keeps his footing. Hani gradually increases the flow of water until it is cascading down the soldier's head and shoulders and the bucket is empty. They do this several times, and then Hani reaches into his rucksack, grabs one of the spare loincloths he has been collecting on his rounds, dips it in the bucket and begins scrubbing in tight circles, starting with the soldier's head and making his way down his back and chest. It would have been easier and more fragrant with a brick of the olive-oil-and-yarrow soap they make by the caskful in the valley. He passes the cloth to the soldier, who washes his own groin, buttocks, and left thigh, then gives the cloth back to Hani. They work together to slowly lower the soldier back to his seat on the parapet. When Hani has finished with his calves and feet, the soldier's eyes close and his shoulders sag in exhaustion. Hani would have liked to rub oil into his skin, which is pink and raw, but thinks it's probably best to wait until morning and let him rest. Slowly, slowly, they ease him off the parapet and onto the robe, in which he wraps himself snugly. He's asleep in moments.

Hani goes fishing again in the morning, again with great success. On his way back from the river, he rounds the stone barrier that guards the gate and stops dead in his tracks. There's movement in the shadowy area just inside the gate, and with the early-morning sun in his eyes it takes him a moment or two to understand what he's seeing. But then there's no mistaking it — there by the gatehouse door stands Arinna, legs akimbo, shading her eyes with the palm of her left hand as she waves at Hani with the right. She's gone before he has a chance to call her name.

SHE'S ALWAYS BEEN a fast runner for her age, but she's just a little girl and incapable of being chased without squealing with laughter, so she should be easy to find. In the few seconds it takes Hani to race through the gate and plunge into the maze of narrow alleys within, she could have zigged and zagged in almost any direction, or hidden herself in a dozen shadowy corners, but he's confident that he knows her well enough to second-guess her choices and run her down as he has done countless times in games of turtle. He tears deeper into the bowels of the city, turning this way and that as his instincts guide him, never slowing and never ceasing to call her name. And if he still can't find her he will loudly sing her favorite lullaby about the baby who dwelled in darkness and she will burst into tears and come forward, as she must. He stops to catch his breath and listen for telltale giggles or hiccups, which often overcome her when she's overexcited. He hears nothing but the breeze wheezing through loose roof tiles, and his own animal panting.

It is only now, with his blood thumping in his ear, that Hani comes to see that he has never truly believed that he would ever find Arinna. Yes, he's told himself again and again that she can be found, that she will be found, and that she has been looking for him all this while just as surely as he's been looking for her. He's always told her that he would never let anything bad happen to her, and that's not something she would forget if she was in distress. But if he's being honest with himself, hasn't he always understood, without ever putting it into words, that his chances of finding her alive in a place like this are stupidly slim? Hasn't he always suspected, in his heart and in his dreams, that he has probably already walked right past her body without realizing it? When you were a kid playing hide-and-seek, you always had that excited feeling inside, like a cloud of butterflies in your tummy, that the person you were looking for was just around the corner, behind the bush, under the table. That feeling was the whole reason you played. But Hani has never felt that about Arinna. He has never sensed that Arinna was just around the corner, not once since he left the valley in search of her. But he does now. He believes now, and with every bellow of her name as he races to catch her, he believes even more that she has been alive, here, around the corner, all this time.

"The household god cries, Who awakens me?" he sings. "The little baby woke you up!"

But why did she vanish? Why did she wave and then run away? Surely she must know that he has traveled half-way across the world to rescue her, and surely he is the one person on all this earth she would want to greet with open arms? This is hardly the time for silly jokes; Arinna of all people would get that. What can she be thinking? He calls her name, again and again, and he can hear his voice strain to penetrate every empty room of every empty hovel in the abandoned city, and then melt away like an ebbing wave into the sand. He can feel the salamanders in the fissures of the rampart and the swallows in their nests and even the vultures on their updrafts pause and raise their heads and wonder at the cry echoing down the empty streets into dusty silence, but he can't feel her presence.

"You've scared the nanny and kept the wet nurse up. The household god has had no rest, his wife has stirred all night!"

He makes his way back to the well, where the soldier awaits him in confusion and alarm. He has heard the shouting, coming first from one side, then from another, rising, falling, despairing, wilting. He knows the name Arinna, and even if he doesn't know exactly who she is he could guess easily enough, so when Hani begins to gesticulate wildly and pepper him with questions he can't possibly understand, it doesn't take him long to figure out what has happened, more or less. He shakes his head—he has seen nothing and heard no one. The look on his face is crestfallen, heartbroken. He reaches up and grasps Hani by the wrist, urging him to sit and rest, but Hani won't. The soldier tugs on his arm, more insistently this time, and shakes his head again, and now Hani sees a different message in his gaze that he has no interest in deciphering. He runs off without another word and spends the next hours crisscrossing the city high and low, including the grim places he has vowed never to return to, and tracing the full circumference of its impassive walls. He shouts, he sings, he calls her by her secret name, which he has never spoken out loud before. When he has exhausted himself, he collapses in the shade of an alley wall and hangs his head, panting, his mind empty. But after a while it begins to stir anew to the lullaby that he has been singing through the deserted streets of the city all day. He allows himself to float on the surface of the melody as if it were a gentle river current, but when at last he opens his eyes he finds, to his disgust, that he has been sucking his thumb like a baby.

He returns to the well in midafternoon, hot and miserable. He dumps a bucket of icy water over his head, falls asleep weeping, and wakes up ravenous. Neither he nor the soldier has had a bite to eat all day. The fish he caught this morning are lying in the dirt somewhere out near the barrier, and they're inedible by now in any case, so he makes a lentil stew, which they eat in silence. At one point, deep in thought, Hani looks up to find the soldier staring at him with an amused smile. Hani has no idea what's so funny until the soldier glances pointedly at Hani's bowl, and then at his own. Hani has wolfed down his entire meal in the time it's taken the soldier to eat just a small fraction of his. Hani winces. When you grow up with big brothers, you learn to eat fast or to make do with leftovers, everybody knows that. He can hardly believe the soldier would stoop to judging his eating habits, especially at a time like this. The soldier rubs his own tummy and makes an exaggerated frown, but Hani has never in his life suffered any digestive problems because he eats too fast. *Next thing you know,* Hani thinks, *he's going to tell me to slow down, it's not going to run away.*

"Shut up, you're not my mother," he says, only half in jest, and sticks out his tongue.

At dusk, the soldier lights two oil lamps and offers to teach Hani more sound pictures, but he doesn't have the strength or the heart for it. Instead, he breaks out the knucklebones and plays one-two-three-four while the soldier watches. He knows the soldier can't understand a word he's saying, but he tells him the whole story of how he became the best knucklebones player in the valley through tireless practice and ruthless exploitation of his opponents' weaknesses. No one could beat him. Word of his godlike talents spread far and wide until even the grown-ups knew of him. One night, his father took him aside to tell him how proud he was, which was a first for both of them. Hani was not at all used to enjoying his father's approval of anything he did or said, so he remained alert and watchful for all the possible ways it could go sour. But Father turned out to be so proud that he did something totally out of character, something unlike anything he had ever done for Hani before or would ever do again. In secret, he had made an inventory of the hind shanks of every sheep that had been slaughtered in the valley that fall until he had collected six of the most well-proportioned, perfectly balanced, sturdy knucklebones that had ever existed — five to play with and a spare in case one was lost. He had polished each one to a glorious glow, then finished them with a fine glaze of pine resin and linseed oil, and made a brushed lambskin pouch with braided horsehair drawstrings to store them in. He presented them to Hani publicly at the harvest festival and everyone agreed that they were the most beautiful set of knucklebones they had ever seen and fit only for a champion. *Beautiful* was the word they used, so Hani remembered it. And as the owner of these beautiful knucklebones, Hani did them proud. His game went from strength to strength and his fame echoed from valley to valley. Many was the boy who offered him great wealth for the knucklebones, and there were a few who tried to steal them, but there was nothing in the entire world that Hani would ever take for them, and there still isn't.

When he's finished his story, Hani holds out his hand so the soldier can see for himself that he has told the truth.

It's as if the soldier has understood every word he has said, because he accepts the knucklebones with all the awe and reverence they are due, turning each one to catch the flickering lamplight and reflect it back in amber stardust. And even though the soldier is a rich man's son and has surely seen his share of exceptional knucklebones, he is properly dazzled. And then he tosses them onto the outstretched robe, picks up the jack, and proceeds to play a masterful round of under-the-arch at the speed of someone half his age. He's not as fast as Hani but his skills are impressive, and Hani laughs and claps in admiration and surprise. He's especially happy because very few people recognize the great importance and benefits of knucklebones. There are not many things in life that are so valuable and so versatile. Kids play games with them, men gamble with them, and women and priests use them to see into the future. To Hani's way of thinking, a friend who can be trusted to appreciate the awesome truth about knucklebones is a friend worth keeping. If a boy could choose who he wanted as a brother, Hani would choose someone just like that. He is careful to retrieve the knucklebones and stow them securely away when the soldier is done.

Back in the gatehouse, he lies awake listening to the sounds of the night, most of which are drowned by distant jackals wailing like the inconsolable baby in the lullaby. That night he dreams that he goes to Kur for an audience with the goddess Lelwani, who rules over the spirits of the dead. Kur is a dark cave so deep and wide the vaulted roof

looks like the night sky, but Lelwani is beautiful and compassionate and knows just why he has come. Before he can
say a word, she coos in her goddess language and Zizi and
Arinna appear before him. He instantly recognizes that they
are spirits because although they laugh and talk to him, he
can't hear what they are saying and their outlines are fluid and
wavy, as if he is seeing them through a depth of fast-running
river water. Even so, it's comforting to be with them. Now he
will know where to look for them when it's his time to join
them in the underworld. But one thing troubles him — Zizi
has Arinna's dark hair and brown eyes, and Arinna has Zizi's
light hair and blue eyes. He asks Lelwani about it. Her voice
is full of wind and honey, so he knows the answer is going
to be something so sad that he will not want to hear it. He
wakes up before she can tell him.

Hani's mother used to say that dreams come through
two gates — some through the gate made of gold, the others through the gate made of mud bricks. Unless you know
which gate a dream came through, you can't know if it's true
or false. The dream Hani had last night was a message, but
what did it mean and who sent it? Hani has always been
taught that the gods send messages to humans in many
different ways that can be interpreted only by oracles and
priests. You have to be careful trying to figure them out
for yourself because you don't know the sender's intentions.
There are more than a thousand gods on Mount Hazzi. Was
the message sent by a god who loves you or a god who wishes

you harm? If the god loves you, he's probably trying to tell you something important—something that is about to happen to you, a danger that is stalking you, a treasure that awaits you if you know where to look for it. But if the god hates you, the message is very likely to be a lie intended to set you astray and put you in the way of someone who means to hurt you. Only a holy person in direct communication with the gods can say for sure which it is. But what kind of god hates an eleven-year-old boy? It's scary, not knowing why bad things happen, especially when there's no one around to talk it out with. Scary and lonely. People think that an eleven-year-old is almost a man, but sometimes what it feels like is being a river with two beds that changes course every time one season gives way to the next.

There's just the palest wisp of moonlight outlining the frame of the window; it draws Hani from his bed and out into the night. He crouches in the corner of the gateway, in almost the exact same spot where the child he saw this morning stood and fled. A warm, salt-heavy breeze rolls in from the distant shore. The night sky bristles with stars, each one a living god, every single one of them knowing where Arinna is and not telling. And the sea down there, aglow and pulsing at the bottom of the plain, it, too, is swarming with nymphs and sirens who could tell him what he wants to know if they chose to. Even the jackals up the hill, prowling and howling over their maggoty carrion, know something he doesn't. How he wishes Ansa were here to advise and gladden him; how he wishes anyone who loves him were here. It's been so long since he has heard a voice. Even in his dream, Zizi and Arinna could not speak to him, because they were dead.

They are dead. If the message in the dream meant anything at all, that must be what it meant. What else could it mean? Zizi and Arinna are in the land of the dead, and they are waiting for Hani to join them. It is the simplest of messages that anyone could understand. Ansa must have known it. It is surely what the soldier was trying to tell him earlier in the day. You don't need an oracle—any idiot could interpret it. Any idiot but Hani.

But if Arinna is in the underworld, who was that he saw by the gate today? It's true, he saw her only for a flashing instant, but it never occurred to him that it was anyone but Arinna. Same height, same spindly legs, same hairline cropped like a boy's. What are the chances that some other little girl, just the same size and shape as his sister, would suddenly appear, wave to him, and run away? What are the chances that such a little girl has been roaming around the ruined city all this time and he hasn't seen or heard the slightest trace of her? What are the chances that such a little girl could slip away without a trace, without a sound, as if she were a ghost? And even if it was Arinna, how did she get here? Who is with her? Arinna could not possibly have survived all this time by herself. If not Father, who has been taking care of her, and who has been listening to

Hani call out for her day after day and keeping her hidden from him?

In the dream, she had Zizi's hair and eyes. That was very strange. What could it mean? When he saw her by the gate this morning, she was too far away for him to see the color of her eyes, but the hair, maybe it was light brown and maybe it wasn't. He knows what he wanted to see, and he also knows that sometimes you see what you want to see and hear what you want to hear. But if he can't trust his eyes to see what is before them or his ears to hear what they're being told, how can he ever distinguish what's real from what's not? Maybe he can't and never has.

Maybe the child he saw this morning was Zizi's ghost, sent from Kur to break the bad news to Hani. Or maybe it was Arinna's ghost, come to say her final farewell. Maybe it was neither of them but some sort of mischievous sprite that takes human form and delights in confusing and misleading mortals for its own entertainment. That happened to a boy from the valley, Hani can't remember his name, who was lured away from his siblings by a water nymph in the form of an Egyptian cat and never seen again. Some people say it was what happened to Zizi. Everybody is in danger all the time, and no one knows why.

Sometimes it feels that everyone Hani has ever known is a ghost now. Arinna, Zizi, Huzzi and Arnu, Mother, Father, his aunt Nikkal, his uncles Sharruma, Pudu, and Tarhun, his grandfathers Hapilzi and Panku, his grandmothers

Kammanu and Alzawatna, so many cousins; friends like Alaksandu and Tudha, whom he has known his entire life; Labarna the carpenter and his naughty wife Kanza, Kurunta the farmer and Kuzi the miller and his son Zidanta. They are probably all dead by now and he'll never see them again. He can barely remember what some of them even looked like. Were they ever real in the first place? Were they all just figments of his imagination? Maybe the child Hani saw this morning was a figment of his imagination, too. The truth of the matter is, if you look at it from a certain angle, it's more likely that Hani himself is dead or a figment of his own imagination than it is that Arinna is still alive. Maybe all those folk were always ghosts, living in the ghost world that existed before the war began. People talk about that world as if it overflowed with milk and honey and all good things, but what proof is there that it even existed? Grown-ups lie about everything, so who's to say they weren't lying about that, too? The old world could easily have been a figment of their imagination no more real than Arinna was this morning when she stood and waved in the shadow of the gate.

The crescent moon retires, the stars fade and wink out, the sky pales and the dawn begins to stretch her fingers at his back. Down at the far end of the plain, the first rays of the sun caress the fringed waves rolling to shore. Hani is wrung out, but he feels as if he's figured something out, though whether it's for better or for worse it's too early to tell. Sometimes you work something out in your head before you even realize there was a problem. His mind, his thoughts, feel lighter, as if they have shed a burden. He mixes flour, salt, oil, and water for the breakfast bread, and because it's dawn and the fish are expecting him, he makes for the river and spears two fine specimens. By the time he has cleaned and cooked them he has even come up with a brilliant idea, and he hurries to the city to share it.

The wounded soldier is practicing on his crutch, limping shakily up and down the plaza around the well. Now that he has discarded his tunic and dresses like Hani in nothing but a loincloth, like a commoner, his wound is fully visible, on the mend yet angrier and uglier than ever. The olive oil he has been rubbing into it every day has not made it any prettier, but it does appear to be giving him less pain. He flaunts his newfound mobility, which is modest but clearly a source of great satisfaction. The soldier is pleased with himself and wants Hani to be pleased, too, so Hani laughs and claps until the practice session is over. They eat and wash, but instead of leaving for the day as he usually does, Hani sits down beside the soldier and retrieves from his bag the clay tile on which he cooks the daily bread and the charred spit on which he roasts the fish. He demonstrates his new idea by using the charcoal at the tip of the spit to make drawings on the tile; they are far clearer than those inscribed in the dust and just as easy to erase. Hani explains that when he has the chance to collect more tiles, he will be able to save the drawings instead of erasing them, which will help him to memorize and practice them whenever and wherever he wants.

The soldier is impressed, and Hani proceeds to draw the symbols of his own name on the tile. The soldier looks at him quizzically, distrustful. *What are you doing here with me?* he asks him with his eyes. *You should go look for Arinna.* When Hani returns his gaze steadily and firmly, the soldier erases *Hani* and draws *Arinna.* Hani shakes his head, erases *Arinna,* then points to the blank space.

The soldier teaches him ten drawings that morning, one of each for *sa, se, si, so, su* and *pa, pe, pi, po, pu.* The lesson reminds Hani of when he and Arinna first began working out the details of their secret language. It's a private adventure shared only by the two of them, but it can get confusing. If it wasn't clear before, it's clear now that he and the soldier do not speak the same language. Sometimes the soldier points to certain things—a storage jar, the sky, fire—that apparently contain those sounds in his language but not in Hani's. When Hani and Arinna were teaching themselves their language, at least they were able to talk to each other and agree on the thing they were trying to name. But when Hani points at a house, or a door, or the well, or the sky, or his foot, the soldier makes drawings that sound nothing like Hani's words for these things. The soldier can't utter them and Hani can't pronounce them. It's going to make things very complicated and very slow, but Hani is good at this and rarely needs to be shown the same drawing twice. By the end of the day, he knows all the important body parts in the soldier's language, and the soldier knows them in his, and at dinner he learns the drawings for lentils, beans, chickpeas, onions, bread, olive oil, water, fart, burp, and piss. The word for *poop* turns out to be the same in both languages.

Now that the soldier can walk, sort of, he's eager to see more of the city. The next morning, shambling along cautiously and deliberately, Hani shows the soldier his lair in the gatehouse and offers him the bed. They eat a breakfast of fish (*"Ikiti!"*) and bread (*"Posomi!"*) in the shadow of the barrier beyond the gate, with the entire plain and bay spread out before them. It is empty and barren yet a source of childlike delight to the soldier, who has seen almost no sunshine in weeks, except at midday when it briefly penetrates the gloom of the crossroads where he has been recuperating. Hani sees it all afresh through the soldier's eyes and shares in his pleasure, despite the fact that this sun-bathed landscape is the very place the soldier and his army left their homes and families and sailed across the sea to destroy. But Hani doesn't care about any of that anymore. The war is over and the old world has been laid to rest and he and the soldier are building the new, one symbol at a time.

Even so, over the next few days Hani finds himself constantly looking over his shoulder, waiting for the ghost of Arinna or Zizi to make itself known to him. It doesn't come easily or naturally to him to give up on something he has sought for so long, especially since he's not even sure that he's ready to give up on it. Still, when you really think about it, it's not so very hard to believe two different things at the same time — that they are gone and that they remain. It even makes more sense that way, somehow. If Arinna should decide to pay another visit to the land of the living, he will not be afraid of her this time. She does not want to hurt him or blame him; she just misses him, as he misses her. At night sometimes, with the soldier sleeping across the room in the gatehouse, there will be something in the wind huffing across the plain or blundering in the angles of the ramparts that wakes him up to ask a question, and once at their quiet lesson he and the soldier look up to see a jackal round the corner and stop to assess them with a knowing eye. Maybe that was Arinna and maybe it wasn't, but in any case there are no further communications from the underworld after that. Which is just as well, because the sight of a frowzy jackal or the sound of a siren call riding the breeze can still be enough to bring Hani to the verge of tears.

There are dozens and dozens of sound symbols to learn, and Hani is not always able to guess what they mean, but after a day or two he finally comes to understand that some of the drawings represent things instead of sounds, and then it all begins to come together and make more sense. Some are easy, because they look just like the thing they point to. The picture for *man* looks exactly like a man. Likewise the pictures for *woman, horse, ewer, arrow, dagger, wheel.* But the drawings for *honey,* or *flour,* or *wine,* or *oil,* or *ox* are complicated, random, and difficult to memorize, and there are hundreds of them. At night, Hani studies his tiles by lamplight and finds himself so excited about learning his new language that he can feel his heart beating in his chest. Also, it's easy enough when the soldier is able to point to the object he's naming, but it's a lot harder when that object isn't there and he has to try to act it out. He can just about manage to get down on his hands and knees and pose as an animal, but what animal is he? There's no way of telling since the soldier can't even say "moo" or "baa." Hani has to go through all the different barnyard calls to identify the creature in question, but even that doesn't always help. How does a ram sound different from a ewe, or a sow from a boar? How do you perform the difference between a trout and a carp, or bronze and gold, or a bird and a bat, or an olive and a fig? And even when Hani guesses correctly, the soldier has no way of knowing that he's got it right. He assumes he must be getting a lot wrong, but the soldier is a patient teacher, taking pleasure in Hani's successes and winking at his failures. Gradually they begin to understand one another on a primitive level, and in the end they both seem to agree that making mistakes is a small price to pay for the pleasure it gives them to be able to talk to each other.

Hani learns that the soldier comes from a place called Puro, a city on the shores of a distant sea whose king Nesuto lives in a great palace. The soldier's family owns a vast farm that is rich in wheat and supports hundreds, or maybe thousands—this is unclear to Hani—of head of sheep and horned cattle. His father Pilipu is a chieftain of his tribe and has three sons, of whom Hani's soldier, Rewonida, is the youngest. When the war began many years ago, Pilipu and his two older sons joined the army and sailed here to the city, leaving Rewonida in charge of the estate until he was old enough to fight. By the time he came of age and set off to join them, his father and two brothers were already dead and the war was almost over. Rewonida was wounded in the fighting on the day the city was stormed and overrun, and was left behind when the victors sailed home with their spoils. He's the same age as Huzzi and calls Hani "little brother." Hani asks him about the Akhillisa and brilliantly impersonates a drooling, slouching monster that eats children and dismembers grown men, but the soldier has no idea what he's talking about.

To the best of his limited ability, Hani describes his home and family. He tells him mostly about Arinna, of course, but also about all the others: Father, Mother, Huzzi, Arnu, Zizi. He tells him about Ansa and promises to bring him to her grave when he's able to walk that far. He tells him about the farm and the things they used to grow on it, and about the famous horses that have been raised and trained in the valley. And as he does so he comes to see all the ways his life and the soldier's life were so alike, even though one of them is a princeling and the other a peasant. Sure, there are the cattle, the sheep, the wheat and barley fields, the olive groves and the seasonal rhythms of the farm. But the one thing they have most in common is that almost everyone they know is dead, their farms lie in ruins, they have no way to get home, and they have no idea what comes next. With every other man in his family dead, the soldier is now the chieftain of his tribe and will have to find his way home sooner rather than later to claim his inheritance. But his kingdom is at least three seas away and it could be years before a ship ventures into port anywhere near this ruined city, and even if it does he has no way to pay his fare and nothing to prove that he is who he claims to be and that he can pay handsomely when he reaches his dominions. Hani thinks that the soldier should come with him to the valley and help rebuild the farm while he waits to find a way home to Puro. The soldier could pretend to be Huzzi, who as the eldest son has first right to inherit his father's position as foreman. There will be few locals left who remember Huzzi, and in any case no one will challenge the soldier's identity if Hani claims him as his brother. Hani thinks that people will naturally recognize the soldier's nobility and leadership and that, together, the two of them will have a real chance to make something new and better from the ruins. Hani thinks that once the soldier has put down roots and invested his youth and his strength in the valley's future and prosperity, he'll have no reason to want to return home, where no one but some distant cousins and nothing but strife and power struggles await him. And when he makes the decision to stay, instead of being Hani's pretend brother, the soldier will become his real brother, and with the soldier's learning and Hani's superior hand-eye coordination, there's almost nothing they can't do together. When the time is right, Hani will somehow have to find a way to convey all this to the soldier and convince him that it's the right thing to do, but for now he will keep it to himself. It's a lot to ask someone to do so much imagining in one try.

Instead, he applies himself to memorizing all the drawings the soldier is willing to teach him, and how to put them together in the right order to say something complex and meaningful. He has begun to see as he learns that this system is not what he imagined it was before he learned how to use it. Yes, it's something private that only he and the soldier share, but unlike his secret language with Arinna, anyone can learn it and put it to all sorts of uses. As a king, you could use it to draw up your laws and send them anywhere in the world for your servants to carry out. As a cattle farmer or a horse breeder, you could let someone far away know exactly what you have for sale and what it costs, instead of having to drive your livestock great distances to some customer who may or may not end up buying them. As a priest or a poet, you could record lengthy prayers or songs instead of having to learn them by heart or spend years teaching them to your apprentices. As a teacher, you could set down the things you see, the events that take place and the people who participate in them, so that they will never be forgotten. Hani thinks that maybe if some of the kings and warriors who destroyed the city had known about disasters like this that had happened in other places, because someone had written down accounts of them, they might have thought twice about doing what they did, because who would be stupid enough to start a war like this if they knew how it would end?

They also work hard together to get the soldier back on his feet. It's not only the wound but all those days he spent bleeding, half-starved, and dehydrated that make his recovery slow going at first, but he's young and strong and more than willing to work through pain to get where he wants to be. As an aristocrat who has been trained in the warrior arts since early childhood, he's also disciplined and well skilled in a whole regimen of stretching, strengthening, and arms-bearing exercises that he cycles through every day in the morning shade of the city wall, where swallows swoop in and out of the nests they have built under the hoarding. Using the spears that were abandoned in the gatehouse, as well as wooden swords fashioned from scrap wood, Hani learns at his side through mimicry, with occasional corrections when his form is off. The soldier tries to teach him the basics of spearing and swordplay, but his limited mobility makes his instruction awkward at best. With drawings and some clumsy miming, he shares his opinion that Hani will make a fine soldier one day. As evidence, he points to the shadow of downy fluff on Hani's upper lip and chin, which Hani didn't even know was there. Hani is having great fun with the war games, and he doesn't want to hurt the soldier's feelings, so he keeps his deep distaste for soldiering of any kind to himself, but to make up for his disloyalty he remains as cutthroat in their daily knucklebone tournaments as he has ever been.

When they begin to run low on provisions, Hani starts to think the time has come for an expedition to the stockpile he left at the foot of the citadel ramparts when he last raided the palace kitchens. He gathers his rucksack and all the bags he has collected and explains his mission to the soldier, who indicates his strong desire to accompany him. It's no more than a league's distance from the gatehouse, but it will be by far the longest journey the soldier has attempted since he began walking again. Hani is not certain that the soldier is up to it, and he certainly won't be able to carry anything heavy, but Hani doesn't even consider saying no. There's something he wants the soldier to see.

The fastest way to get there is along the winding street that leads from the south gate through the center of the city to the ramp at the foot of the citadel, but that would take them directly past the marketplace, which Hani has no desire to ever see again. Instead, they take the roundabout way, skirting the inner circumference of the city wall as it curves north and then west and finally meets the citadel ramparts on the inland side of the city. It is here, on a lane that Hani has not visited before, that they see a child's hand poking up through a sewer grate and waving at them. On closer inspection, they find that the arm belongs to a little girl, but she is not waving it; her body is being fought over by two tribes of rats, and it is their tug-of-war that is making the arm flutter. She is only one lonely little corpse among so many, but they lift the grate and pull her from the sewer. She's not in good shape. Hani scouts the local houses for something to serve as a shroud, but finding nothing he and the soldier build her a makeshift cairn from the surrounding rubble. She's so small it takes no time at all. Before they close her in, Hani takes the onyx ring from his pouch and places it on her withering finger. She can show it to Arinna when they meet. They move on through the upper city toward the citadel.

The corpses scattered at the foot of the ramp and along the main granite-paved avenue to the palace are in an advanced state of decay and unavoidable, but Hani looks neither to the right nor to the left and hustles the soldier along as fast as he is able to move. The soldier allows himself to be herded and does not choose to linger. It's quite possible that he knew some of these corpses when they were his fellow soldiers, but nobody who knew them would recognize them now. In the plaza, the soldier pauses to gaze thoughtfully at the shattered remnants of the giant horse, and offers Hani a bitter tilt of the head before moving on.

It's all uphill to the palace, and flight upon flight of stairs once you get there, but the soldier takes them gamely. Even in its wretched state the palace is a place of awe and mystery to Hani, but the soldier eyes its marble floors and massive pillars appraisingly, as if comparing it in his mind to other homes he has visited. Hani is unable to explain what they are about to see — he has seen it twice now and can't describe it adequately even to himself — but his excitement is contagious and heightens the anticipation. When they finally reach the dining hall, with harsh late-morning sunshine stabbing through jagged gaps in the partially collapsed roof, the soldier responds just as Hani had hoped he would. His mouth falls open and his eyes light up, his gaze leaping like a frisky lamb from one scene to the next. Hani points out the little girl who resembles Arinna, and the soldier nods and laughs silently. At last, he leans back against the edge of the table and quietly, avidly, scans the painting top to bottom, left to right, then back again. His gaze is intense but a little hysterical, like that of a starving man eyeballing a lavish banquet. Hani recognizes the hunger, but he also knows that the soldier understands what he's looking at better than he himself ever will. This city is not the soldier's homeland, but it's his world — the world of privilege, power, wealth, and learning. These people were his enemies — they spoke a different language, wore different clothes, ate different food, and prayed to different gods — but they were closer to him in many ways than someone like Hani can ever be. When Hani looks at these scenes and these people, they are as freakish and as alien to him as the king in his distant capital. When the soldier looks at them, he sees his friends, his family, his estates and property, his ancestors. And when he finally turns to smile at Hani with tears in his eyes, Hani can't help thinking that maybe in these paintings he has found the faces of people he has known and loved. Maybe he's longing for his farm and his loved ones, and the paintings remind him of how far away they are and how long and winding the journey home will be.

Before they leave, the soldier points to one corner of the painting that Hani has not noticed before. It shows a ship at dock, its mast raised and crew at their oars. On the dock stands a group of women and children waiting to board, their arms bound at the elbows behind their backs, their necks tethered to a long, slim pole that keeps them in single file. Soldiers stand guard behind them, swords drawn, to prevent any of the prisoners from escaping. Hani understands why the soldier has brought this scene to his attention, and he supposes that there could be some comfort in believing that Arinna was abducted as war booty and that she is still alive and living across the sea as a slave in the palace of a rich man who treats her kindly, but it's still too hard to look at and he turns his head.

Hani leads the soldier out to the terrace so that he can take in the sweeping view of the plain and the sea. No matter how hot it is down there and in the shaded depths of the city's alleys, it's always breezy up here — the kind of breeze to give a king false hope. The entire ruined city lies at their feet, as mud-colored and battered as a beaten dog. Way down there to the west, at the foot of the hill, they can just make out the great south gate where they have been living for the past weeks. To the north lie the bay and the open sea beyond. To the east lie the steep escarpment and the road that led Hani from the valley to the city. It runs straight through broad fields that should be golden with wheat at this time of year but are instead ocher and lifeless, then rises into the rolling hills on the horizon. About halfway between the hills and the horizon, there is a caravan of people, carts, and pack animals making its way toward the city.

THE SUMMER AIR is humid and hot, the north wind that has blown all through the spring has been defeated, and all that lies in the distance shimmers and wavers as if behind a curtain of flame. The caravan appears to be on the small side — maybe half a dozen wagons, maybe thirty or forty people — but it's hard to tell at this distance. Hani guesses it will take the travelers a good two hours to reach the city, and with their heavily laden carts they will need to bypass the eastern escarpment to find a more level entryway, giving him added time to come up with a plan.

Hani and the soldier exchange helpless glances. There's no way to know who these people are or what they're looking for, but Hani goes over the possibilities in his mind. First of all, they're not likely to be stragglers from the invading army, left behind by their comrades in the confusion of the sacking and victory celebrations. The invaders were hardened warriors, but Hani can't see any men-at-arms in the group, mounted or on foot. That could turn out to be wrong too, of course. Also, if they were invaders they'd be coming from the west, not from the east. Likewise, they're probably not members of the defeated home army who somehow escaped the slaughter and are returning, disguised as civilians, to comb through the wreckage now that it's safe. They don't move like soldiers, even disgraced ones. If Hani had to guess, and he does, he'd say they're most likely to be refugees who fled the fighting and have now turned back to reclaim their homes. He has seen plenty of those in the valley over the past months and years, all heading in the opposite direction, away from the city, desperate, poor, and dirty. They, too, traveled at that slow, cautious, weary pace, carrying all their sorry possessions on their backs or in rickety pushcarts, looking for any place that would allow them to settle. They were never allowed to settle in the valley and they moved on, who knows where. Now, somehow, they've gotten word that the war is over and it's safe to go home. If that's the case, there will be plenty more where these came from, and all of them are in for a very unpleasant homecoming.

No matter who they are, Hani believes that it would not be wise to wait around to find out. Even if they're not soldiers, they'll probably be armed with weapons of some kind and on their guard against strangers. And when they see what has been done to their kinfolk and to their city, and the grim work that lies ahead if they ever hope to call this place home again, they're going to be outraged and itching for revenge. It would be smart to stay out of their way and out of sight for some time, and maybe just to consider packing up and moving on altogether. Hani sends the soldier back to the gatehouse while he goes to gather their provisions where he left them at the foot of the ramparts.

With time pressing, the shortcut through the market is the only practical way to get there. The smell has all but vanished. What remains of the corpses are mostly leathery shells collapsed into themselves, aloof and freed from the insult of all they have been subjected to, in death as in life. The skeletons are not yet grinning but they will be soon enough. The maggots, beetles, vultures, and jackals have done their good work, and the market and its occupants look as if they have fallen into a kind of eternal sleep, as if all that was flesh has turned to stone and is being absorbed into the cobbled pavement and tumbled masonry, like some sort of ancient monument — like Tarhuntassa's fortress back in the valley. That, too, must once have been foul with the corpses of those who died for its vanished and forgotten glory. Even as he averts his eyes, Hani almost feels sorry that these slumbering dead and the city streets on which they sleep will soon be rousted, swept away, and taught to forget what has happened here. It would be a kindness if they could somehow remain undisturbed forever, if no one were ever allowed to walk these streets again, but he knows that can never happen. Sooner or later, someone is always going to come along to move the dead out of the way of the living. People do it every day, in their homes and in their minds. Nobody gives a thought to the comfort of the dead, but they, too, have their reasons to demand respect.

At the foot of the rampart, he quickly assembles a heavy bundle of beans and pulses, flour and salt and oil, which he hoists onto his back. This will be far too much to take with them if they have to make a quick escape from the city, but he's thinking ahead in case some of it needs to be cached outside the walls for future use or they need to make a quick break for it. Although the caravan is still far off, he scurries along like a rat, almost doubled over by the weight of his burden in the meager afternoon shade of the city wall, as if the faithless sun itself were following his progress and reporting it to those who are on their way.

Hani reaches the gatehouse before the soldier. He's thinking that if he carries all the food himself, the soldier should be able to manage the blankets and the two spears, maybe one of the waterskins if they take it slowly. He stands at the gateway and casts his eyes across the plain. The problem will be which way to go. To the north, toward the bay, and the west, toward the coast, there is almost no cover of any kind. If they go that way they will be visible and vulnerable long after the caravan reaches the city, especially at the snail's pace at which they will have to travel. If the caravan circles the city to the north, as Hani did when he first got here, he and the soldier can head east, concealing themselves in the shadow of the southern ramparts. They could try fleeing to the south, but Hani has no idea what awaits them there. He seems to remember old stories about a string of powerful and aggressive port cities down that way, every one of which will be wary of outsiders arriving at their gates unannounced, especially one with all the bearings of a barbarian invader. So that's not an attractive option either. At a pinch, they might consider heading south, in the direction of Seha, then turning east and trying to find their way to the valley through the mountains that block the way, but Hani isn't sure he can chart such a complex course through the roadless wilds, and he doubts the soldier has the strength for such an arduous journey anyway. Even so, as chancy as it seems, it may be their best bet. He will put all these options before the soldier this evening and together they will make the right decision. And whatever decision they make, it will mark the birth of their new and everlasting brotherhood.

The soldier takes so long to get back that Hani has begun to worry. When he finally does, he's exhausted and in pain, and in no mood to discuss their predicament, let alone plan an escape route. All he wants to do is wash himself down and get off his feet. When Hani tries to get him to focus on the situation, the soldier shrugs it off as if it were a minor inconvenience of no urgency. Hani thinks this is a funny attitude for an invalid who may be in imminent danger, but he drops it for the time being. He fixes some supper, moving the fire into an abandoned hovel to conceal and dissipate the smoke and to shield it from the late-afternoon thunderstorm building over the sea. The soldier turns in to sleep almost as soon as they're done eating. Hani stays up to stand watch from an angle of the gateway, sheltered as the storm breaks overhead. He keeps his ears alert for unusual sounds and his eyes peeled for firelight, but the night is quiet. The travelers must have made camp on the far side of the city, wary of exposing themselves to unknown hazards so late in the day. They will certainly not be exploring by starlight, abundant and crisp as it is following the cleansing storm.

Hani is not sure how he should feel about this latest development. After all these weeks thinking of himself as the last survivor, of imagining that the world itself had come to an end, he knows that he ought to be glad that he has been proven wrong. The world has been severely wounded but it is not dead yet. It will survive, and it may even be that in his own little way it is he, Hani, who has helped it get through its most perilous moment, who has nursed the faint, tentative heartbeat that has carried it from collapse to reawakening. Anybody else would be grateful. And if Arinna, and Father, his brothers, and all the rest of them are gone, the other thing he has learned is that the world is reborn every time you remember those you have lost, so *goodbye* doesn't mean quite the same as what it used to mean. That, too, should console him and help him carry on in whatever new life lies in store.

But he also feels as if something important was stolen

from him the moment the caravan lumbered into view. This is his city now, his world, his life. He seized it when no one else wanted it and he has made it his own, sharing it with only one other person who thinks and feels as he does. He knows there was never any real chance they were going to be left alone to claim the ruined city for themselves, even if they could, but it was here that he first began feeling that the old world had finally begun to loosen its grip and that there might be something new in store, and better. Whatever it is, it would never have happened if things had gone on the way they were going, and that has somehow made the ruined city a home in a way the valley never was. He doesn't really understand it, but there's something in him that wishes the world had stayed ended. He can hardly admit it to himself, but it suits him this way. He likes it the way it is, and everything that would have made it unbearable to someone else — the hunger, the fear, the loneliness, the uncertainty — is exactly what he likes about it. When they were children playing their little game about changing the future, isn't this what they had in mind? Isn't it kind of exactly what they were trying to imagine without knowing it — the world ends and everyone who made you feel miserable and scared is gone and you are the only survivor? How did they know, those dumb kids who had never been anywhere or seen anything, that it would feel so good having the whole world to yourself? And so yes, maybe he's a little resentful that this opportunity has been stolen from him, that now he's going to have to move over and make room for others, strangers, grown-ups, more of the same people who got it all wrong the last time, and who will almost surely get it all wrong all over again. Mothers will go on dying and fathers will go on bullying the weak. Brothers will go on taking up all the room and leaving nothing for anyone else. Children will go on hurting animals. The poor will go on being born and toiling and growing old and dying as ignorant and resentful and incurious as the day they were born. Kings will go on making wars and being murdered by their sons, who will become kings and be murdered by their sons in turn, as regular as the passage of the sun through the skies and the seasons through the year. Nothing will change. But it could have all changed, if only that which was destroyed could have stayed destroyed and that which had been left to Hani could have remained Hani's. So in the end he has to think that he's a little sadder than he is happy. If only it could be just Hani and the soldier, the soldier and Hani, forever and ever.

In the light of dawn, Hani finds the soldier out by the barrier, staring back toward the city, where a narrow column of smoke is rising above the rampart. The newcomers have made camp in the citadel. If they are looking this way, they can see Hani and the soldier right now. Hani sits down beside the soldier and together they watch for signs of activity, but there aren't any. Hani wonders if the soldier is thinking what he himself is thinking, but he doesn't know how to ask.

Over breakfast, Hani lays out his position and their

options as he sees them, as best he can with his bungling command of the symbols and a lot of pointing and pantomime. They can't stay here, he tells the soldier. They've been lucky so far, but it's only a matter of time before they're discovered, if not by these people, then by those who will come after them. And then what? Maybe they're good people and maybe they're not, but either way the two of them have no need for anyone else and are better off not waiting to find out who the intruders are. They can only make things worse just when Hani can feel them getting better. That could never have happened in the old world crawling with strangers and trespassers. *It can only happen,* he tells the soldier, *in the new world that you and I are making for ourselves, if not here in the ruined city then somewhere else, somewhere away.* Hani isn't sure how much if any of this gets through and how much of it has got tied up in his thoughts, but his basic message is simple. *We're ready to go. Let's go now, before it's too late. Let's go. I have a valley. I have a farm. We have a farm. It's waiting for us. Let's go.*

But the soldier shakes his head. He will not go. He was never going. He makes it clear that these are the people he has been waiting for: if not these, then anyone who can take him to a place where there are boats and sea captains who know the way to Puro. He must return home, where he's needed and where his people are waiting for him. It could take years, but that makes no difference. This place is not his home, nor is it Hani's. The soldier wants to go home, and he thinks Hani should go home, too. There is nothing else to say on the matter. Hani scratches out a terse message in the dust. The soldier looks at it and frowns. He thinks Hani has made a mistake, that Hani doesn't know the right drawings to say what he wants to say. But Hani has not made a mistake. He tells the soldier in words what he has just told him in writing. *You are my home.* The soldier shakes his head and points to the west. *Let me come with you.* The soldier shrugs, to Hani's confusion.

Hani spends the rest of the afternoon sitting in the river under a sky of bronze, watching storm clouds swell along the coast and over the bay. The water is barely waist-deep but it will do. He came down here to catch fish for supper, but for the first time in his life he finds that he doesn't have the heart to kill anything. Today should have been a very good day to kill fish, to kill them lustily, even to kill more than he can eat, which is not his way. But that's not how it is. Instead, he sits facing downstream where the fish come to feed, at a seam between the main current and an eddy where the riverbank widens. The fish face upstream directly in front of him and look as if they're talking to him. "I lie here among you, oh fishes," he tells them. "Lick the blood from my wound and gloat over me." But the fish just stare and talk. It's funny until it isn't, but even when he tries to chase them away by churning the water with his hands and feet they return to their chosen spot within moments. How stupid fish are, and stubborn! All he has to do is get up and turn around if he doesn't want to look at them, but that feels like too much work. He tries shouting at them, but either they do not hear him or they are ignoring him, and anyway his raised voice sounds pathetic and slight on the open plain, whereas when he whispers it's almost like the fish are gathering in to listen. If Ansa were here, she would say something like, "They have no idea what you're saying. They're just happy not to be eaten," and Hani would nod as if he understood. If Arinna were here, she would sit next to him in the icy water until her lips turned blue and her teeth began to chatter, but she would remain at his side and she wouldn't move a muscle until he did. He imagines putting his arm around her shoulder and rubbing her back until the circulation returns, and it's almost as if she's there with him. Later, when the storm clouds begin to mass and grow livid, he retreats to the lee of the barrier outside the south gate, but the rain doesn't come.

Hani can hear the soldier approach before he sees him, because of his limp. He's hidden behind the barrier but the soldier finds him immediately. His leg is still stiff and sore; he can walk okay, but it takes him forever to sit, hissing and panting like an overheated dog. Hani finds himself growing impatient and peevish, and he turns his head away when the soldier finally sinks to the ground. The soldier sighs with relief but makes no move to break the silence between them. They sit like this, close but not touching, for some time. They watch the clouds breast the shoreline, carry the plain, and sail on inland, to spend themselves elsewhere. Hani wonders if the storm will make it all the way to the valley, and again he feels a knot of resentment toward the soldier twist at his gut. What would the soldier say if Hani told him he wanted to go with him to Puro? Hani thinks he would say yes, but he's not so sure he wants to go. Puro is even farther from home than it is here. From here, at least, Hani knows the way home. The soldier pokes him in the shoulder and tries to tell him something using hand gestures and body language. Hani doesn't get it, so the soldier smooths out a patch of dust between them and begins to write, but at that moment a gray wall of rain suddenly descends before them and obscures all sight of the bay. Its approach sounds like an army of horses galloping across the plain, and in a moment it has engulfed them, warm and heavy and roaring. The few symbols that the soldier has had time to draw in the dust are washed away. So too, the thundering rain purges his thoughts and softens his heart in a way that the river did not.

He's thinking about Arinna and Ansa. You think you know somebody until you realize you don't so much. He thought he knew them inside out, but the fact is they were both always puzzles to him in ways that he hardly wanted to admit, maybe because it is easier to pretend that you understand the way things are than to accept that the souls you love are strangers to you. Arinna had her many quiet moments, even when he and she were together, playing or talking, and he knew better than to interrupt them because it could make her sulk or cry. Who knew what she was thinking in those moments? He once asked her, and she didn't even know herself, or else she wouldn't say. And even though Hani knew her better than anyone, at those moments her mind was as closed to him as the deepest caverns of the mountains. And as for Ansa, how often did she express an opinion or offer advice that he could really claim to have followed? Basically never. She was a donkey and she didn't talk out loud, and even when he was convinced that she was communicating wisdom and guidance there was always the suspicion that it was all in his head. And the only reason he knows this about them now is because they're gone and no longer adding to the confusion with their presence. They were like an object, say a frog, that you hold so close to your eyes that you can't see it, but when you put it down and step away it comes into focus. You can't step away from someone you love and some-one who trusts you while they're still right in front of you and they still need you, so you can never see them clearly for who they are. But if you can't know anything even about the people you love the most, then what's the point? You might as well just be a carp in the river — point yourself upstream, open your mouth, and see what swims in.

He turns to the soldier, who is staring thoughtfully out across the plain, his braids soaked and fraying, a stray fringe plastered across his forehead. How could Hani ever have imagined that he knew the soldier and understood what was in his heart? When you don't know someone you always start off thinking he's just like you. That's only natural if you think you're a normal person. If you trust yourself, you'll trust him. If you don't know what you want, you won't know what he wants. If Hani himself doesn't know if he wants to go to Puro, why should the soldier know? If Hani doesn't trust himself, why should the soldier trust him? Hani knows the word for *home* in his own language, and now he knows it in the soldier's language, and they don't mean the same thing.

The truth is, the people you meet are always not like you and you always don't know the first thing about them. That's not their fault, or yours, but it's a problem that a few drawings in the sand and a few hand gestures aren't going to solve. It's a problem that's not going to be solved because to solve it you need to be able to talk to each other in the same language, the way he and Arinna used to do, and Hani is beginning to think that no two people in the world, or what's left of it, speak the same language. The complications always start when you think you're speaking the same language, that you understand what the other person is saying and that the other person understands what you're saying, and it turns out no one ever understood anything at all.

Hani rises and goes to lie down in the gatehouse. When he wakes up it's early evening and he finds that the soldier has left him a bowl of lentil stew and a loaf of bread. The lentils are rewarmed leftovers from the day before. The bread is fresh baked, but it's burned on one side and the soldier has forgotten to add salt. He tries eating but his heart isn't in it, so he gets up and goes to look around. The soldier is nowhere to be found, but from outside the wall Hani can see a fire flickering behind the battlements atop the citadel rampart. He watches it for a long while as if it were an eclipsing moon or a long-haired star. He wonders if the soldier is up there with them, sharing their food around the fire, tending compassionately to their tales of woe, and in a dream that's halfway between sleeping and waking he hears him charming the travelers in a voice that rises like apricot nectar from his throat.

Hani is familiar enough with the geography of the city by now that he has little trouble locating the encampment. He conceals himself behind the crumbled stonework of a perimeter wall. A vigorous fire is burning on the portico of a ruined villa in the citadel, high above the ramparts; a ring of jagged stones serves as a makeshift hearth. A family warms itself by the blaze, sitting on rugs and sheepskins arranged in a semicircle on the marble paving stones: a father, a mother, two daughters, and a son, the children all younger than Hani. They are dressed in clean, white linen and delicate sandals; a purple cloak is draped over the father's knees. The children laugh and joke quietly with each other as their mother watches over them. At one moment, she leans across to brush the boy's cowlick from his brow and kiss the tip of his nose. The boy blushes and his sisters tease him, tousling his hair and tickling his ribs. A retinue of servants in tunics and loincloths sees to their needs, ferrying platters of food and drink from somewhere inside the villa. A guard armed with a spear and a sword stands in the shadow of a column a short distance away, but he snaps to alert and draws the sword when Hani steps into the circle of light. The children fall silent and their mother draws them to her, encircling them with her arms. The father assesses Hani with a keen eye. He stands, and the cloak falls to the ground.

"If you understand what I am saying, come forward and join us. You can put down the knife," he says quietly, not in the least alarmed. "If you do not come forward, we will assume you do not speak our language and that you pose a threat."

Hani comes forward, keeping the fire between the family and himself, and drops the flint blade into the dust at his feet. The father watches him a while longer, then smiles.

"Ishara," he says, "make our guest comfortable. Tutha, food, drink."

A servant girl appears at Hani's side, bearing a woolen rug that she places on the ground before him. When he has taken his seat she produces a jug and a bowl and gestures for Hani to hold out his arms. She pours cool water from the jug over his hands, catching it in the bowl, then offers him a drying cloth. She steps aside, and a boy takes her place, setting a low table at Hani's side bearing platters of steaming bread and grilled meats sprinkled with barley, including a thick slice of stuffed goat paunch, Hani's favorite. A different boy offers him a bronze goblet of mixed wine. The platters appear to be made of silver, and the dark gems inlaid into the bronze capture the glowing flame in their hearts.

"Eat, stranger," the father says. "You can tell us about yourself once you've had your fill."

The more Hani eats, the hungrier he seems to get. He tries to eat slowly, with dignity, but he can't—it's not clear whether the servant hovering at his shoulder is there to offer more if he eats it all or to remove the platter before he's finished, so he's taking no chances. He can feel the family watching him eat, especially the children, but he doesn't care what he looks like and they always lower their eyes if he tries to catch their gaze. It doesn't matter—he knows very well what they see when they look at him. In the end, he's allowed to finish everything, but the platter is not replenished. The servant girl returns with the jug, and Hani cleans his lips and fingers.

"I am Kammama," the father begins. "This is my home. Or rather, it was my home, and it will be again. We left the city over a year ago, when it became clear the Ahiya would eventually win the war. We have been living in Percote ever since. We have returned to rebuild what we can. We are the first, but there are many more like us making their way home. Now tell us your story, boy. Don't be shy. You are our guest."

"My name is Hantili, sir. I am from the east. I came here to find my sister, but I think she's dead or taken as a slave. I don't know what to do next. I'm traveling with a friend. He will tell me what to do."

"We met with your friend earlier today. He came to see us."

"You talked to him?"

"He doesn't talk anymore, as you know. But we used to trade with the Ahiya before the war. They speak our language, we speak theirs. They read our writing, we read theirs. I talked, he wrote."

"What did he say to you? Did he talk about me?"

"He's desperate to get home to his farm and his people. We made a deal with him. He will work here as our steward and foreman for three years, and then we will send him home at our expense."

"But he's your enemy."

"We know his family. We used to send them copper and horses. They sent us ox hides and olive oil. They were our partners, and so they will be again. That is the way of the world. And he told us all about you."

"What did he say about me?"

"He told us you have lost everyone and everything. There are a lot of children like you in this country now — too many. We will need every single one of you if we are to rebuild our city and our wealth. Would you like to come with us? We can care for you."

"Come with you? You mean, join your family?" Hani

steals a quick glance at the mother and the children, who are eyeing him with mild curiosity.

"In a sense, yes. What can you do?"

"Well, I can swim. I can whistle. I'm a crack shot with a sling. And I'm a famous knucklebones champion. I can teach you," he says, turning to the boy, who looks away.

"Good for you! But do you have practical skills? Working skills?"

"Oh, I...well, I can harness a mule and steer a cart. I'm still too little to work with oxen. And I can groom donkeys and horses."

"A groom, eh? Can you braid a mane?"

"Yes, sir."

"Yes, that could work. A groom. We'll have plenty need of pack animals soon enough when it's time to clear the streets. Yes, I like that. Why don't you stay with us and help out? You'll have clean clothes and a roof over your head. Simple food but all you can eat. You'll be safe. And in fifteen or twenty years, after you've worked off your debt, you'll have the greatest gift of all — your freedom, and a patch of arable land to call your own. You'll still be young enough to start a family of your own to make up for the one you've lost. How does that sound?"

Hani doesn't even need to think about it. "That sounds great! I'd love it, thank you so much, sir! Let me just run down to where my stuff is and I can be back first thing in the morning."

"No need to get your things. We have all new things for you here."

"My knucklebones, sir. I could never leave my knuckle-bones behind." Hani bows to the father, bows to the wife and children, and then turns and disappears into the night.

IN THE MORNING, the soldier wakes him with a shake of the shoulder and a hopeful smile. He widens his eyes and bobs his head as if he's urging Hani to pretend that all that has come to pass was only a flight of fancy. Hani wishes that were only so. He suspects that the soldier wants to introduce him to his new friends and to encourage him to keep an open mind to whatever they might propose. Hani's mind is anything but open. If the soldier is willing to barter away his own freedom for a boat ride that's his own business, but Hani wants nothing to do with these people in their gleaming white linens. He is shocked and insulted that the soldier thinks so little of him. How could he not know? If their positions were reversed, Hani would not be so quick to turn his back on the boy who had saved his life — a perfect stranger to whom he owed not a single thing. That's right, Hani saved his life and made himself responsible for the soldier forever, and this is how he repays him?

But Hani has never been very good at keeping the flames of wounded outrage blazing for long. He always wants to believe the best of the people he meets, even when they disappoint him. He would like to believe now that the soldier could still come around to his way of thinking and change course before it's too late. Maybe he lied to the stranger's face just like Hani did. It's always possible, too, that the soldier doesn't even know of the intruders' plan to enslave Hani. So Hani decides that he will accompany the soldier wherever he asks him to go, but the newcomers will find no forgiveness in his heart.

As they leave the gatehouse the soldier grabs Hani by the wrist and directs his attention to where the buskins sit waiting as patiently by the threshold as a cat by a mousehole. The soldier makes it clear that he's offering them to Hani as a gift, but Hani turns his nose up at them. The soldier scowls, confused, and Hani softens because he knows full well he will never ever get another shot at such magnificent footwear so long as he lives. He steps into the buskins and the soldier teaches him the proper way to lace them up. When this is done they admire their joint handiwork, and even Hani has to admit that the buskins look pretty good on him. The folks at home would never believe it if he showed up out of the blue in these.

As they exit the city, the soldier does not turn right, as

he would if he were circling back toward the citadel. Instead, he heads straight across the plain, striking out southwest and abandoning the trail that leads to the ford and the bay beyond. As they proceed farther and farther from the city, it becomes clear that this part of the plain was not part of the battlefield used by the clashing armies, and they wade through meadows of wild grass punctuated by the occasional stunted beech. Hani could easily outpace the soldier, but he remains five steps behind him at all times. At one point, the soldier stoops to pick up an object from the ground, which he offers to Hani. It's a leather helmet, decorated with rows of boar's teeth and lined with felt. Hani finds it ugly and useless and hands it back. The soldier shrugs and tosses it into the grass. They reach the river at a spot far upstream from the ford; it's narrow and deep here and must be swum at a sharp angle if you don't want to be swept away. Every so often they're forced to clamber over rough stone walls half hidden in the grass, relics from a long-ago time when this entire plain was partitioned into individual fields for cultivation. At last they reach a dusty path running parallel to the ridge that cuts the plain off from the coast. Here and there the roadbed is littered with the detritus of war—broken chariot axles, a shredded linen corslet, half a wicker shield—but the serenity of the morning is interrupted by nothing more disturbing than the thrum of cricket song. In short order, the path veers to the right through a cut in the ridge, and suddenly they hear the clap and hiss of the surf.

They stride through the remains of a destroyed village, and the beach and the sea come into view. It's nothing like the enclosed bay visible from the city. It is truly open sea, nothing but some distant clouds out far beyond the strand. It's stunning, incomprehensible; it looks exactly the way Hani imagined it would look before he ever saw it. He would like to stop and mark the moment, or take a cooling swim in the turquoise waters, but the soldier maintains a steady pace, not fast but intent, his pain apparently forgotten for the moment. The path carries them down the shore, separated from the beach by a ribbon of rustling sedge. To the right is a low headland, and at its knuckle a modest, rounded hill that, as they approach, reveals itself to be a newly raised barrow, a huge one, overspread with a carpet of young grass. The only sounds are the lapping of the waves and the urgent cries of gulls. The soldier leads them to the foot of the barrow where it kisses the base of the promontory, and stops before a boulder set into the slope.

Only it's not a boulder but a face of flat granite framed by a simple border of repeating spirals. Within the frame are hundreds, maybe thousands of sound drawings of the type that the soldier has been teaching Hani, arranged in tight horizontal lines that fully cover the face of the granite, except at the center, where there are only two words, one above the other, carved in symbols much larger than the rest. The soldier reaches out to the slab with the fingertips of his right hand and lowers his chin as if in silent prayer or remembrance; when he is done he points at the first word, made up of four drawings, and looks at Hani. Hani sounds them out.

"A-ki-me-u?"

The soldier points at the third symbol.

"A-ki-ne-u?"

He points again and leaves his finger touching the stone.

"A-ki-re-u?"

The soldier lowers his finger.

"Akireu," Hani confirms. "What is it? Is it a man?"

The soldier points at the word beneath.

"Pa-ta-ro-to-lo?"

The soldier points at the fourth drawing.

"Ko?"

The soldier nods and sweeps his hand over the granite.

"Akireu. Patarokolo. Who are they?"

The soldier crouches and draws four new symbols in the sand at his feet. Hani knows what these symbols mean because he himself has written them within the past week.

"A-de-ri-fo. Brother. Brothers? Your brothers?"

Down on his knees, the soldier reaches across the space between them and pulls Hani to his chest. His torso heaves, once and again, and Hani can feel hot tears on his shoulders. It goes on and on, in complete silence, so long that the tears begin to pool in the crevice between Hani's back and the soldier's arms. The soldier cradles Hani's head so closely in his hands that Hani's own tears are forced sideways against his cheeks and splash into his ears, and Hani doesn't even know why he's crying. Hani has seen grown men cry before, and of course he's seen every kid he's ever known cry at least once, but this is something different. In Hani's experience, a man or a child cries for himself, his own pain or loss, whatever it may be, but the soldier is crying like a woman; it's a sluice that can't be turned off because he's crying for the whole world, about the whole world. When Hani's mother died, his father cried for himself and himself alone, inviting the people around him to offer comfort and soothing words. When Zizi died, his mother could not be comforted and did not invite comfort, because she was crying not for herself but for every mother who had ever lost a child. The depth of her despair was so obvious, even to her own surviving children, that no one dared to come near her; she cloaked herself in sorrow the way a doomed warrior dons his armor, taking no pity on his loved ones as they beg him not to go to battle. The soldier is crying like that. He's clinging to Hani in his grief, but he's somewhere else now; he has no idea that Hani is still in his arms, in these minutes he doesn't even know where he is. Out of the corner of his one unobstructed eye, Hani watches the waves roll in, pause, then roll out again, and notices that they sound like someone breathing in their sleep.

As Hani's mother eventually stopped weeping so too does the soldier, and as he awakens to his surroundings he loosens his grip on Hani's upper body and slumps against the granite, the side of his head pressed against the forest of engraved symbols. Hani holds his hand and waits patiently until his breathing has quieted. After a minute or two, the soldier wipes his nose on his forearm and lifts his head, offering Hani an apologetic smile and a rueful chuckle. The ground at the foot of the marker is littered with granite chips. Hani finds a good sharp one and uses it to scratch a crude box on the stone face next to the engraving. Within it, he etches the three symbols that form Arinna's name and, below that, the double figure for Zizi's. And below that, the horsehead drawing used for *horse,* because he doesn't know the one for *donkey.* He's reminded of the day he first came to the city and was amazed to see writing and pictures etched directly into the living stone, and now here he is doing it for himself! He shakes his head in disbelief at his own genius. He can hardly imagine all the things he would know how to do if someone had told him about learning when he was little.

It's hot under the midday sun, with barely a breeze off the water. Hani beckons and the soldier follows him across a stretch of gorse and broom to the beach of bright white sand and the edge of the water. Hani crouches to remove the buskins, unties his loincloth, and slips the knucklebone pouch from his belt. He empties it into his palm, then returns everything but one knucklebone, the spare, to the pouch. When the soldier catches up to him, he makes two fists and hides them behind his back until the soldier forces him to hold out his hand. Hani drops the knucklebone into his outstretched palm and with all the strength in his two hands squeezes the soldier's fingers shut around the knucklebone so that he can't return the gift. *The knucklebone is me,* Hani wants to tell him — one day when he's back at home in Puro, the soldier will look at it and remember Hani better than if he had painted his name in symbols ten hands tall. And when Hani is back home on his own farm in his own valley, a small part of him will be all the way across the sea in Puro.

Hani turns back to the sea. The waves here are bigger than those in the bay but they don't intimidate Hani, who dives right in, stretching and pumping his arms and legs as his chest glides just above the seabed. The water below the surface is so clear and calm that he can see all the way to where the bottom falls away into darkest purple. In the distance is a pulsating school of small fish, shimmering silver with a bright red stripe down their bodies. Underwater, the rhythmic breathing of the breaking waves is both muffled and intensified. Hani stops moving and allows himself to sink to the bottom to listen to it. The sound of the tide raking the sand in one direction, then raking it back in the other, is like a lullaby sung by a turtle. *Assiyatar.*

When he breaks the surface, he's surprised to see the soldier still standing at the water's edge. He waves to him, but the soldier shakes his head and Hani understands that he doesn't know how to swim. That is too pathetic, especially for someone who has sailed halfway across the world. In the valley, even children who are barely old enough to walk know how to swim. If Hani had the time, he would teach the soldier how to swim like a child, so freely you don't have to think about it, like running or breathing. Everyone should know how to swim like a child. A vision of the two of them swimming like children in the river below Kuzi's mill flashes before his mind's eye, but he dismisses it. Hani will go home and teach someone else how to swim. The soldier will go home and someone else will have to teach him how to swim.

Hani holds out his hand, the soldier takes one step, two, and stops. He starts again as Hani wades toward him, absorbing the breaking waves on his back, and they meet where the water reaches Hani's waist. Hani takes his hand and they go out farther, where there is only a gentle swell as the waves pass and the water comes up to Hani's shoulder. Hani demonstrates how to float on your back, his arms and legs stretched wide open and his chest inflated and arched, and the soldier tries to emulate him, leaning back until his upper body is horizontal. He lifts one foot off the bottom, then balks. Hani places the tips of his fingers on the soldier's back and uses his other hand to coax him to raise both legs, and then to gently support them, and the soldier is afloat on the surface of the water.

"Good," Hani says, and then, "Now breathe. You can do it."

And he can, after briefly going under and coughing up a lungful of water. In a minute or two, he's floating on his own, more or less confidently. His braids gleam in the sunshine and bob all around his head like strands of pondweed, but his face—eyes closed, lips pursed, and water streaming down his cheeks in the sunshine—reminds Hani most of all of a water lily in full bloom. Hani pulls his hands away and floats beside him, closing his eyes against the bright sun. They bob together, rising and falling with the swell, and with his ears underwater Hani listens to the sounding sea.

ACKNOWLEDGMENTS

Deep and sincere thanks to my editor, Josh Kendall, who saw unplumbed depths to this story and plumbed them, and to the staff at Little, Brown who made the publishing process so pleasant and easy: Kayleigh George, Elizabeth Garriga, Gregg Kulick, Liv Ryan, Arik Hardin, Amy Schneider, Susan Buckheit, and Katherine Isaacs. Very grateful to Will Staehle for the gorgeous and astonishing jacket design. Thanks to my beloved agent, Gail Hochman, for her patience and guidance. To my early readers Herzlia Clain, David Schwab, and Shelley Sonenberg for their invaluable insights and candor. To Sophie and Cora Browner for being the very best role models. Most of all, to Judy Clain for her love, wisdom, and friendship.

ABOUT THE AUTHOR

Jesse Browner is a novelist, translator, and essayist. He was born and lives in New York City.